THE MYSTERY OF THE
CRANKY
COLLECTOR

Who wants to harm Jeremy Pilcher? Who doesn't! The ornery book collector has more enemies than the Three Investigators can shake a stick at. So when the nasty old man is kidnapped, the detectives don't know whom to question first.

The solution to the kidnapping is buried deep . . . in Pilcher's vast collection of books, in his secret computer files, in his mysterious past. The Investigators must search through each in turn to find the missing man.

But the more they learn about him, the surer they are of one thing—the cranky collector really asked for trouble!

The Three Investigators in

THE MYSTERY OF THE
CRANKY
COLLECTOR

by M.V. Carey

BASED ON CHARACTERS CREATED BY
ROBERT ARTHUR

RANDOM HOUSE NEW YORK

Library of Congress Cataloging-in-Publication Data:

Carey, M.V.
   The Three Investigators in The mystery of the cranky collector.
   (The Three Investigators mystery series ; 43)
   "Based on characters created by Robert Arthur."
   SUMMARY: When an ornery book collector disappears, the Three
Investigators break into his secret computer files in search of clues
and gradually uncover his mysterious past.
   [1. Mystery and detective stories] I. Arthur, Robert. II. Title.
III. Title: Mystery of the Cranky Collector. IV. Series.
PZ7.C213ThK   1987   [Fic]   87-4723
ISBN: 0-394-89153-8 (pbk.); 0-394-99153-2 (lib. bdg.)

Manufactured in the United States of America

   2   3   4   5   6   7   8   9   0

CONTENTS

A WORD FROM HECTOR SEBASTIAN

Greetings, mystery fans!

Once again I've been asked to introduce an adventure of those busy young detectives, the Three Investigators. This time the boys rescue the meanest guy in town from a fate he probably deserves. Along the way they unravel a four-hundred-year-old mystery from South America that involves a historical villain and a lost treasure. That should be enough excitement for anyone, but there's more. A disastrous party, a telltale computer, and a haunted house keep the sleuths on their toes.

That's all I'll say about the mystery for now. No sense in giving the story away. But those of you who haven't met the Three Investigators before will want to know something about them.

Jupiter Jones is leader of the team. He's a

plump boy. Some would even say he's fat. No matter. He's brainy and determined and way ahead of everyone else when it comes to deducing the truth from a slender clue.

Pete Crenshaw is the Second Investigator. His strong suit is physical coordination. He's the most athletic of the three boys—and the one most nervous of ghosts.

Bob Andrews, an all-round type, is in charge of records and research. Quite often his sleuthing takes place in the library, where he comes up with some amazing information.

The Investigators all live in the seaside town of Rocky Beach, California, not far from my own home in Malibu, and not far from Hollywood. They work out of a secret headquarters in The Jones Salvage Yard, an enterprise run by Jupe's Aunt Mathilda and Uncle Titus.

Now that you've met the boys, turn to page 3 and read on.

HECTOR SEBASTIAN

THE MYSTERY OF THE
CRANKY COLLECTOR

I
THE MEANEST MAN IN TOWN

"Watch out in there!" said Harry Burnside to the three boys. "That old grouch will come down on you like a ton of bricks if anything goes wrong."

Burnside was usually a jovial, joking sort of person, but now he was scowling. "That skinflint!" he said. "He wouldn't cough up enough dough so I could get decent uniforms for you guys. Jupe, did you try that jacket on before you took it from the rental place? It doesn't fit you *any*where!"

Jupiter Jones shifted the tray of cheese puffs and rumaki that he was holding and looked down at himself. He was a stocky boy, and the white waiter's jacket he wore barely buttoned across his ample midsection.

"It was the best I could do," he told Burnside. "They had a bigger jacket, but it cov-

3

ered my hands. I thought I'd probably be using my hands today."

Pete Crenshaw stood behind Jupe with a tray of carrot sticks and dips. His white jacket was so short that it barely reached his waist, and his wrists stuck out of the sleeves. The thing made him look like an amiable scarecrow.

Bob Andrews, the smallest and normally the neatest of the three boys, wore a jacket that was too big everywhere. He had rolled the sleeves back so that his hands were free to carry his tray. For the first time in his life he looked sloppy.

Harry Burnside sighed. "Okay, it can't be helped now. Just go out there and pass the cheese stuff and the dips to the guests and keep out of old Pilcher's way. If you drop anything he's liable to take your heads clean off!"

Burnside held the kitchen door open, and Jupiter, Pete, and Bob carried their trays out. They started to circulate among the guests in the living room. The room was crowded with people as well as with old, uncomfortable-looking furniture and shelves full of curios. French doors opened onto the garden, letting in the June warmth but no breeze. All three boys felt hot and stiff and nervous. Each clutched his tray with great concentration, careful not to spill anything or bump anyone and so attract the wrath of the terrible-tempered Mr. Pilcher.

The boys had never met Mr. Pilcher, but they had heard a great deal about him, and nothing they had heard was good. Various business publications rated Pilcher as one of the wealthiest men on the West Coast, worth uncounted millions. His neighbors in Rocky Beach, and the shopkeepers who dealt with him, rated him as the meanest man in town. People said he was so stingy that he still had ninety cents of the first dollar he ever made.

When Harry Burnside hired the boys to help serve at the Pilcher party, they had seen that Burnside was desperate. He was the newest and youngest caterer in town, and the party at Pilcher's home was the first big job to come his way. He had had to scramble to get together a staff for the affair, and Pilcher had made the task doubly difficult. According to Burnside, Pilcher had acted as if he were in a contest to see how cheaply he could entertain his guests. When Burnside protested, he had simply remarked that doing it for less was just the name of the game. He had haggled and bargained about costs and had insisted that there was no need to pay waiters and waitresses a penny more than minimum wage. As a result, the girls who were setting the tables in the garden were recent graduates of Rocky Beach High; the bartender was a trainee at the Cup of Cheer Bartending School in Los Angeles; and the dishes were being washed by a drifter named Ramon whom Burnside had found at the New Hope Mission.

The waiters who passed the hors d'oeuvres were Jupiter, Pete, and Bob.

The boys had agreed to help out not because they needed the money. Money was always welcome, of course, but the boys were more curious than broke. As members of The Three Investigators, the only junior detective agency in town, they were always looking for mysteries to explore, and Jeremy Pilcher counted as a mystery. He was almost a legend in Rocky Beach. He was also almost a recluse. The boys couldn't pass up the chance to meet him and to see the inside of his house. It was a decrepit old pile on Mockingbird Lane, surrounded by a dank tangle of garden. The place was so dreary that the townspeople said it was haunted.

The party that Burnside was catering for Pilcher was in honor of Pilcher's daughter, Marilyn. She was the old man's only child, a sheltered heiress who had been sent to boarding schools. As a result, Rocky Beach kids had never had a chance to get to know

her. Now she was a student at an eastern
college, and Burnside had told the boys that
she would announce her engagement at this
party. Burnside had also confided that Jeremy Pilcher disapproved of his daughter's
fiancé, and that he hated the whole idea of a
party.

"He said it was just throwing good money
away," Burnside had told the boys. "He's
going along with the act because the daughter nagged him into it. He figured if he gave
her the party, and even let her hire some
musicians, she'd be satisfied for a while. He
said he's going to work on her to see if she
won't get tired of the fiancé and give him the
heave-ho before the wedding day arrives.
Then Pilcher will find a nice Wall Street
wheeler-dealer type for her. Or maybe he'll
bring her into his business. I have a feeling
that's really what he'd like."

As Jupiter passed the cheese puffs to the
chattering guests, he wondered which of the
men could be Pilcher. Most of them were
middle-aged. Jupe knew that Pilcher was
older—seventy at least. And most of the men
were well-tailored and looked as if they pa-
tronized expensive barbers and posh health
clubs. That did not jibe with Jupe's mental
picture of Pilcher.

But any of the girls who laughed and

shouted to be heard above the thumping and twanging of the trio of musicians might be Marilyn Pilcher. She might be the redhead in the white dress. She might be the brunette in pink. She might be the blonde in the blue dress who was chatting with the faded-looking woman in gray silk. The woman seemed distressed. When the blonde turned away for a moment to say something to the smooth-faced young man at her elbow, the woman glanced toward the ceiling. Her hand went to her throat.

Jupe looked up. A cobweb hung in one corner of the room. Also someone had recently squashed a bug on the wall nearby.

The woman in gray frowned with distaste, then looked quickly away. Jupiter tried not to smile. Being a waiter was in some ways harder work than being First Investigator of the detective team, but the job sure had its amusing moments.

Suddenly, just as the musicians finished a set, one of the young waitresses dropped a glass outside. It shattered on the flagstone path in the garden.

Immediately Jupe knew which of the men was Pilcher. He was the tall, very thin one with the shaggy gray hair and the black suit worn shiny with age. The man came charging out of a corner. With an angry cry he started toward the garden. For a second Jupe thought he was going to seize the waitress and shake her. At the last minute he caught himself. "Watch what you're doing, you little—"

He stopped, leaving the sentence unfinished, and glowered at the girl outside. Then he wheeled about and marched past his guests, heading through the dining room toward the kitchen.

"Dad, take it easy, huh?" The blonde in the blue dress darted after Pilcher.

"Marilyn?" The gray-gowned lady put out a hand as if to restrain the girl. But then she stopped and let her hand drop. She looked at the smooth-faced youth next to her. "Jim, really! That man!" she said.

The young man trotted after the girl. "Marilyn, wait. Mr. Pilcher, the girl didn't mean to drop it. Mr. Pilcher? If you'll just—"

Pilcher paid him no attention whatever. He pushed the kitchen door open and stood framed in the doorway. Jupe had the impression the old man was drawing in his breath so that he could really deliver a blast about the clumsy waitress.

Jupe stood still and watched. He saw Harry Burnside flying back and forth from the stove to the table, furiously arranging food on platters. At the sink the dark-haired drifter was swirling dishes through the suds.

"Burnside, get that incompetent girl out of my house!" Pilcher shouted. He obviously did not care who heard him. "And if you think I'm paying for that glass she just broke, you're wrong. I'm not!"

"Dad, will you cool it, huh?" pleaded Marilyn Pilcher. "You'll get your angina all stirred up. And you're going to ruin my party. Dad, come on! Please!"

Marilyn Pilcher put her hand on his arm and tried to coax him out of the kitchen doorway. Jeremy Pilcher had not finished shouting, however, and he wouldn't be coaxed.

The dishwasher looked around at Pilcher. He scowled as if protesting the uproar. For an instant he and Pilcher stared at each other. Then the dish he was holding slipped from his hand and crashed to the floor.

The party guests had given up all attempts at conversation. They stood awkwardly, pretending not to notice Pilcher's tantrum. In the silence the smashing plate sounded like an explosion or a car crash.

Pilcher gasped.

"Dad, if you just wouldn't get so mad!" cried Marilyn Pilcher. "It can't matter if . . . if . . . Dad?"

Pilcher suddenly bent double and clutched at his chest.

"Oh, I told you so!" wailed his daughter. "I warned you! Ray! Ray, come quick! He's going to faint!"

She grabbed the old man around the waist, but he was too heavy for her. His knees buckled and he sagged to the floor.

2
LOCKED IN!

A dark-haired young man dashed in from the living room. He and Harry Burnside hoisted Jeremy Pilcher off the floor. Marilyn Pilcher got a chair from the dining room and put it under the old man.

"Oh, Dad, I told you this would happen!" The girl was almost crying with anger and anxiety.

"Who's his doctor?" A stout woman who had a take-charge air swept into the group near Pilcher and put a finger on his wrist, feeling for a pulse. "Where's the telephone?" she demanded. "I'll call his doctor."

"No!" gasped Jeremy Pilcher. "No doctor! Don't need a doctor."

The dark-haired young man bent toward Pilcher. "Mr. Pilcher, we're just trying to—"

"I said I don't need a doctor, you idiot wetback!" croaked Pilcher.

12

The younger man did not react to this abuse. He did not even seem to hear it. Watching, Jupiter wondered whether Pilcher was in the habit of insulting his friends this way.

But then Jupe heard one of the guests murmur an explanation to a companion. "The young guy is Ray Sanchez," he said. "He's Old Man Pilcher's personal secretary."

"Jobs must be scarce these days" was the second man's dry comment.

"Upstairs!" Pilcher ordered now. "Want to go upstairs and rest. I'll be okay in a few minutes."

Ray Sanchez looked around at the guests. His eye fell on Pete, who stood near the buffet table in his too-small waiter's outfit. "You," said Sanchez. "Give us a hand, huh?"

Pete put down his tray and went to the old man's side. He and Sanchez lifted Pilcher from his chair and began a slow, staggering progress toward the front hall where a staircase went up to the second floor. Marilyn Pilcher went ahead of them, and the guests stepped back to let them through.

Jeremy Pilcher felt like a dead weight as Sanchez and Pete lugged him up the stairs. They were both breathing hard by the time they reached Pilcher's bedroom. It was at the front of the house where the windows looked out toward the mountains.

Sanchez and Pete eased Pilcher down onto the bed, and Marilyn bustled into the adjoining bathroom to get a glass of water for her father. When she offered the water, Pilcher just pushed the glass aside. Water splattered across the bedclothes. "Nitro!" cried Pilcher. "Where's my nitro?"

"Right here." Marilyn Pilcher yanked open a drawer in the bedside table and took out a prescription bottle.

"Well, open it, open it!" scolded the old man. "Don't just stand there like a cow!"

"Dad, one of these days I'm going to get my hands on some strychnine—and then won't you be in for a surprise!" She shook a pill into her father's outstretched hand.

"I blocked you on that move," said the old man. "You know good and well what's in my will—if anything funny happens to me you're out on your tail!"

He put the pill under his tongue and lay back.

Pete was embarrassed by this barbed exchange between father and daughter. He began to back out of the room, but Marilyn Pilcher saw and caught him by the sleeve. "You stay here with my father," she ordered. "I have to go back to the guests. Come with me, Ray. I need you to help."

Pete felt a prick of panic. He did not want to be left with this sick, nasty old man. "Miss Pilcher," he protested. "I can't. I'm supposed to be—"

"You're supposed to be doing as you're told." At that moment Marilyn Pilcher sounded much like her father.

"But what if he . . . if he stops breathing? If his heart—"

"He won't stop breathing. It's not a heart attack," Marilyn said impatiently. "It's only angina. His blood vessels have gone into spasm, that's all. His heart isn't getting quite enough oxygen, so he's in pain right now, but the nitro will take care of that. It isn't serious."

"I wish it was you who had it!" snapped Pilcher. "You wouldn't be so quick to say it isn't serious."

"Sure, Dad," said the girl, and she turned and went out of the room.

Ray Sanchez smiled at Pete, shrugged, then went after Marilyn.

Jeremy Pilcher lay still. His eyes were closed. Pete sat down in an armchair near the bed and watched the old man. Pilcher's face was gray except for the places where small veins made purple patterns on his skin. The nose was high and thin, the cheeks were sunken. Pete's gaze shifted to the hands.

They were skeleton hands with the bones clearly visible through the flesh. They were crossed on Pilcher's chest, almost as if the old man were laid out for burial.

The thought scared Pete. He looked away quickly and began to examine the room where he sat. He saw a fireplace that hadn't been cleaned since winter; gray ash was heaped up behind the tarnished brass fender. A brass basket on the hearth held a few sticks of wood and a pile of yellowing newspapers that could serve as kindling. A model ship and a pair of dusty candles in china candlesticks decorated the mantel above the fireplace.

Pete took a deep breath. He was sure he smelled dust. He imagined it drifting from the walls and the drapes, rising like fog from the faded, stained carpeting. Did anyone ever clean in here, he wondered.

A mirror hanging over a big dresser was spotted and yellow. In places the silver had peeled away from the back of the glass. A pair of small armchairs had been set on either side of the dresser; the upholstery on the chairs was faded. So were the watercolor pictures on the walls—pictures of sailing ships and of stormy seas breaking on rocky coasts.

Everywhere there were bookcases. They lined the walls and nudged close to the dresser and crowded the chairs. They were all filled to overflowing. Pete saw paperbacks and hardcovers, small books and volumes so big they had to be put on the shelves sideways. There were papers, too, some stacked in piles, some rolled into cylinders. Here and there manila folders and big brown envelopes had been slipped in on top of the books.

Pete glanced at the bed. Old Man Pilcher appeared to be asleep. His breathing was hoarse, but it was regular and even. The skinny hands no longer clutched each other; they were open and relaxed on his chest.

Pete got up and went to one of the bookcases. He read the titles on the backs of the books. *Bloody Murder* was one. Another was *Shark Hunter*. There was a collection of stories by Edgar Allan Poe and a book titled *Polaris*. Pete slid it off the shelf and opened it. It was a guide for seafarers, telling how to navigate a ship by the stars.

Pilcher let out a sound that was half a groan and half a snore. Pete jumped as if he had been caught doing something forbidden. He slid the book back onto the shelf and waited, watching the old man and listening to the voices of the guests below. How long would the party go on? How long would he be stuck here watching this cranky old codger sleep?

He looked at his hands. They were smudged and dusty. Probably the bookcase hadn't been cleaned for months or even years.

Pete went into the bathroom and closed the door. There were books here, too. They were heaped on a low table between the old-fashioned claw-foot tub and the washbasin. One was a collection of cartoons; another was a copy of a book on atomic energy. Evidently Pilcher would read anything and everything. Jupiter Jones was like that. He was a voracious reader who remembered most of what he read. But it was strange to think that Mr. Pilcher, obviously a world-class grouch, shared an interest with Jupe. Jupe might be sort of pompous and preachy at times, but he wasn't a grouch, ever.

Pete turned on the water and began to wash his hands, using the sliver of soap from Pilcher's soap dish.

Suddenly, sharp and clear, there came the sound of a key turning in a lock.

"Hey!" Pete grabbed a towel and flew to the door. He turned the knob and pulled. The door didn't budge. It was locked tight.

Pete called softly, "Mr. Pilcher? Mr. Pilcher, open the door, please."

No one answered.

Pete rattled the knob. "Mr. Pilcher?" he said more loudly.

Footsteps went away from the door. Pete put his ear to the wooden panels. He could hear the guests talking and laughing downstairs. The musicians were no longer playing. A door opened nearby and the party sounds grew louder.

"Mr. Pilcher?"

Still no one came. No one answered.

Pete felt himself getting warm with embarrassment, with fright. Was Old Man Pilcher mad because Pete was using his bathroom? Perhaps he thought Pete meant to harm him. He might have gotten confused and decided that Pete was a burglar. Had he gone to call the police?

Pete sat down on the edge of the tub and waited. If the police came, it would be okay with him. In fact he would be kind of glad to see the police about now. But then there were footsteps again. They were the same footsteps, and they were coming back to the bathroom door.

Old Man Pilcher must have decided Pete was harmless; he was coming back to unlock the door and let Pete out.

But he didn't touch the door. Instead he

gasped, and Pete heard a scuffling sound as if Pilcher had stumbled, or as if he were struggling with someone just outside the door. There was a grunt, then a thud.

Pete leaped toward the door. He rattled the knob. "Mr. Pilcher?" he yelled.

At that second the rock group down in the living room burst into a number called "Baby, Why Ain't You My Baby No More?" It was very loud, heavy on the drums, with lots of amplification.

"Mr. Pilcher?" Pete shouted, but he could scarcely hear himself. "Mr. Pilcher, are you okay?"

The music thundered on.

Sweating now, near panic, Pete pounded on the door.

Pilcher didn't respond. A heart attack! He must be having a real heart attack, and not just some kind of spasm that wasn't important. He might be dying now, right outside the door.

"Got to get out!" cried Pete. He stamped and stamped on the floor.

No one heard him. No one came.

"Baby, Why Ain't You My Baby No More?" crashed to a conclusion, but there was no period of silence. The band roared right into "Rockin' Rockin' Rockin' All the Night."

Pete pounded the door in frustration. What

can I do? he thought. There's a sick old man out there in need of help. What can I do? What would Jupe do?

"Calm down and use your head!" came the voice of the First Investigator in Pete's memory.

Right! thought Pete, and he slowly looked around the tiny room. His eye fell on the window.

The window! Pilcher had a nice, old-fashioned bathroom with a window. Outside the window a tree grew quite close to the house. It looked like a good sturdy alder— ideal for climbing up, or down.

Pete shoved up the window, then pulled over the table on which Pilcher's bathroom books were piled. Hopping up on the table, he poked his head and shoulders outside.

He looked down. He was at the side of the house. A cement walk lay directly beneath him. If he fell, he would break a leg, at the least. Or an arm. Or he might crack his skull.

But Pete, the best athlete of The Three Investigators, was an expert tree climber. He wasn't likely to fall. And he didn't dare fall.

If I don't get downstairs and find some help fast, he told himself, Old Man Pilcher might die!

3
THE MISSING MILLIONAIRE

Pete went down the tree as quickly as he dared, barely pausing to test handholds and footholds. No one had been in the yard beside the house when he climbed out the bathroom window, but by the time he reached the ground a red-haired girl had appeared. "What a fun way to come down," she said. "Most people just use the stairs."

"Right," said Pete. He didn't bother to explain but simply dodged past the girl and ran to the other side of the house, where the long windows were open to the living room.

The music was still blasting when Pete stepped through a window into the mob scene inside. Guests struggled to talk above the sound of the band. Jupe and Bob were sweating slightly as they valiantly passed trays.

Pete darted through the crowd toward

Marilyn Pilcher, who stood talking to a woman in a gray silk dress. Pete touched her elbow to get her attention. She turned, and when she saw Pete, she scowled. "You're supposed to be with my father," she shouted above the music.

Pete started to explain, then shook his head and beckoned for her to follow him to the kitchen.

As they went through the dining room she spotted Ray Sanchez at the far end of the room. He was hovering over Harry Burnside as the caterer set platters of thinly sliced ham and turkey and bowls of pasta salad on the buffet table. Marilyn crooked a finger at Sanchez, and he followed her into the empty kitchen and closed the door behind him to muffle the noise of the band.

"Your dad locked me in the bathroom," Pete told Marilyn, "when I went in to wash my hands. And a minute or two later I heard a thud. I think he fell. I yelled, but he didn't answer, so I climbed down a tree, and I think—"

That was as far as he got. Marilyn Pilcher ran for the back stairs, and Sanchez strode after her.

The door to the dining room inched open. Jupe looked in. Bob peeked over his shoulder. "What's up?" asked Jupe.

"I think Old Man Pilcher freaked out," Pete told him, and explained what had happened. "The daughter's gone up to check on the old guy."

Jupe looked at the ceiling, then at the back stairs. He started toward them.

"You think you should do that?" asked Bob. "Marilyn Pilcher might not like us butting in if her dad has really flipped."

"If Mr. Pilcher isn't well, his daughter may need help," Jupe said primly.

"Go right up, if you don't mind carrying your head under your arm," warned Pete, but after a moment he started up the stairs after Jupe. He had seen Jupe operate too many times as leader of The Three Investigators. Jupe could hold his own if Marilyn Pilcher challenged him.

Bob hesitated, then followed Pete.

The upstairs hall was a blizzard of feathers. A pillow had broken open there. The crumpled tick lay on the floor, and feathers swirled everywhere. Marilyn Pilcher was wading through them, banging doors open, looking into rooms, shouting. Sanchez wasn't shouting, but he was looking.

"He's got to be here someplace!" cried Marilyn. "Where could he go? There's no place he could go!"

The door to Pilcher's bedroom stood open.

Jupe looked in and saw the impression of Pilcher's body on the wrinkled bed sheets. Tiny flames danced in the fireplace across from the bed, sending wisps of blackened, burned paper up the chimney. Jupe frowned. The day was very warm. Why would anyone light a fire?

Jupe ran to snatch the tongs from the stand beside the fireplace. He tried to rake the fire out onto the hearth, but there were only the brittle remains of burning paper. They fell to bits as soon as the tongs touched them.

"What are you doing?" Marilyn Pilcher grabbed the tongs from Jupe. Her voice was rough with anger. "Why aren't you downstairs passing things? Get out!"

"Miss Pilcher, my associates and I may be more useful to you if we remain," Jupiter said, using his most adult manner. Unhurried, he got to his feet. "We have had considerable experience examining places where unusual happenings have occurred," he explained. "Frequently we have been able to reconstruct events and solve mysteries that have baffled other investigators."

Marilyn Pilcher's mouth opened, but for a moment the girl was speechless. Pete wanted to cheer. Jupe had done it again!

Jupe now looked calmly around. The bathroom door was still closed; an old-fashioned skeleton key rested in the lock. Jupe went to the door and unlocked it. The bathroom was just as Pete had left it, with the little table under the window and the window open.

Jupe removed the key and tried it in the door between the hall and the bedroom. It fit the lock there. "It would probably work in any door in this house," Jupe observed. "Miss Pilcher, before your father disappeared, he locked Pete in the bathroom. Does he often treat his guests that way?"

"Your buddy isn't a guest," snapped Marilyn Pilcher. "He works here, remember?"

"Very well," said Jupe. "Does your father often shut his employees in the bathroom?"

He looked toward Pete. "After you were locked in, you heard a thud. Something fell. You think it was a body? Could it have been Mr. Pilcher?"

"It . . . I suppose it couldn't have been anyone else," said Pete. "There wasn't anybody else here."

"Was that fire burning in the fireplace when you were sitting with Mr. Pilcher?" Jupe asked.

"No." Pete shook his head. "No fire."

"It's a warm day," Jupe observed. "Why would anyone light a fire?"

Jupe looked toward the bed. "One torn

pillow on the hallway floor," he observed. "No pillows on the bed. Was the torn one damaged earlier? And shouldn't there have been two pillows on that bed? Double beds usually have two pillows."

Pete frowned. "I think there were two, but I didn't really notice."

"Of course there were two," snapped Marilyn. "Look, all this Sherlock Holmes stuff is not impressing me. You guys get downstairs and pass the food like you're supposed to, and—"

"Up to a certain point I can tell what happened here today," said Jupiter, ignoring her orders. "It's perfectly clear. Pete went into the bathroom, and your father got up quietly, took the key from the bedroom door, and used it to lock Pete in. Then he burned something in the fireplace."

Ray Sanchez had come into the bedroom. "He must have had something he didn't want anyone to see," Ray said. "He *is* very secretive."

"Ray, don't encourage this kid!" Marilyn scolded. She turned to Jupe. "So he burned something," she said. "Then he tore up one of his pillows, and he took the other with him and he hid someplace. He's ornery. He might do that just to get to me. He's done worse things when he didn't like what was going on—and believe me, he doesn't like what's happening today."

"So he's trying to frighten you?" Jupe prompted. "If that's what he's doing, where is he hiding?"

Marilyn made an exasperated noise and turned away to continue her search. Ray Sanchez joined her. After watching for a minute, the Three Investigators started opening doors too. Marilyn began to protest, then muttered, "Okay, okay! I guess I can use all the help I can get."

The boys saw that the big square bedrooms of the old house were almost uniformly dusty. Most of them appeared to be unoccupied. Some were furnished with beds and dressers, some were empty except for floor-to-ceiling shelves crammed with books and papers.

"Gives you a new feeling about books," said Bob. "Like collecting could be a compulsion, like gambling or biting your fingernails."

"It's a disease," said Marilyn Pilcher. "Believe me, it's a disease."

Books were not the only things Jeremy Pilcher had collected. There were trophies of voyages to far parts of the world—a Turkish fez, a water pipe, a pair of leather slippers that Marilyn told them were from a bazaar in Egypt. There was carved ivory from Africa and there was a tarnished brass lamp that Pilcher had bought in Marrakech. Navigational instruments were jumbled onto shelves beside pencil boxes and old magazines.

"Dad never throws anything away," Marilyn grumbled. "And he won't let anybody clean up here. He's afraid somebody's going to make off with some of his precious stuff."

Marilyn sighed, and the boys felt a twinge of sympathy for her. She had a sharp manner, but with a father like Jeremy Pilcher, she could be excused a great deal. And evidently Marilyn herself had a yearning for order and neatness. Her own room was tidy and prim.

The only other orderly area on the second floor of the old house was the computer room, which was next to Jeremy Pilcher's bedroom. Heavily air-conditioned, it was stark and efficient, with white walls, metal chairs painted a brilliant red, and two computer consoles.

"One of these is set up to interface with the big computer in the office downtown," explained Sanchez. "Mr. Pilcher doesn't care to go out much anymore. He uses the computer to keep in touch. He can give orders to his staff by keying things in on the machine, and he doesn't have to bother talking to people. Besides, it gives him a record so the staff has no comeback if they don't follow orders and they mess things up."

"My dad likes to know where the blame belongs," said Marilyn grimly. "Okay, so he isn't here."

"Is there an attic?" asked Pete.

There was. It contained more books and boxes and souvenirs of the past, but no sign of Jeremy Pilcher.

When they finished searching upstairs, Marilyn turned to Jupe. "Okay," she said. "Where is he? You're such a smart kid, you tell me!"

"We have eliminated all the other possibilities," said Jupiter. "Therefore we must conclude either that he walked down the stairs and out the front door, and no one noticed because the guests were busy talking—"

"I don't think so," interrupted Marilyn. "I could see the stairs the whole time. I think I'd have noticed if he came down that way."

"What about the back stairs?" asked Ray Sanchez. "If he went down the back stairs, he could get to the cellar or out to the backyard."

"Carrying his pillow?" said Jupe.

"Why do you keep talking about that pillow?" Marilyn demanded.

"Because it may be important," said Jupiter.

They went down the back stairs. The drifter who had been hired to wash the dishes was busy at the sink.

"Did you see my father come down here?" Marilyn asked him.

The man looked around. His face showed he was at least fifty, even sixty, but his body was burly and muscular. A dragon had been tattooed on his right forearm. Jupe thought he looked sullen. The man responded to Marilyn's question with a shake of his head, and he went back to his dishes.

Harry Burnside came in from the dining room. "Something wrong?" he asked.

"I seem to have lost a father," Marilyn told him.

The Investigators looked in the basement and found mildew and old trunks and spiders. They went out and circled the house and saw overgrown shrubs and grass that was weedy and lumpy with neglect. Party guests were now eating at the tables that had been set up in the garden, but Jeremy Pilcher was not sitting with them.

At last there was no place else to look.

"So it's like the kid said," decided Marilyn. "He's walked out on me. He doesn't want me to get married, so he beat it. He thinks I'll get so uptight, I'll forget about Jim and my engagement and—"

"Suppose that isn't it," said Jupiter. "Don't forget the pillow. Would a grown man take a pillow along if he chose to disappear? That would be like Linus and his blanket. And don't forget that thump Pete heard. A sound like a falling body. And what about the fire in the fireplace?"

"What *about* that fire?" demanded Marilyn. "And that thump—that could be just ... just part of an act he's putting on. He's capable of it. It's all a game with him. He figures if I get mad enough, he makes points."

Jupiter shook his head. "Isn't it just as logical to conclude that your father burned something in the fireplace to keep it out of someone's hands? And that somebody took him away, using that pillow to muffle his cries?"

Marilyn Pilcher stared at him, her face very white. "You mean he might have been kidnapped?"

Jupe nodded.

Marilyn thought a minute, then finally spoke. "We'd better call the police!"

4
THE PARTY'S OVER

"Your dad disappeared? Really?" The red-headed girl opened her eyes very wide. She had watched Pete climb down the tree, and she had been delighted. Now she was equally amused by Marilyn Pilcher's predicament.

Marilyn was in the lower hall, her hand still on the telephone. She had just called the Rocky Beach Police Department, and the dispatcher had promised to send a car right away.

"It's a game, isn't it?" said the redhead. "Like that party game where somebody pretends to be a murder victim and we're supposed to figure out who did it."

"Oh, shut up, Betsy," said Marilyn. "This is no game."

But the redhead wasn't listening. "We're supposed to figure out where your dad is, aren't we? Or who made him disappear.

33

That's it. Who had a motive?"

"Betsy, you're an airhead," said Marilyn.

The smooth-faced young man who had been talking with Marilyn earlier came from the living room. He looked flustered and annoyed. By keeping his ears open during the afternoon, Jupe had learned that this was Marilyn's fiancé. His name was Jim Westerbrook; he was one of Marilyn's college classmates. The woman in the gray silk dress was his mother. She had flown in with him from Boston just so that she could attend this party.

Earlier in the afternoon Jupe had come upon her running an exploring fingertip across a window sill, testing for dust. He wondered if the lady was happy to have made the trip to California, and how she liked the idea of her son marrying into the Pilcher family.

"Where have you been?" Westerbrook asked Marilyn now. "Everyone's been asking for you."

"I was looking for my father," she said.

"Oh?" he said. "Why? Is he still in a temper? Forget him."

Jupe was hovering nearby, and he winced at Westerbrook's remark.

Marilyn pulled back and glared. "Whether you like him or not, he's the only father I've got," she snapped. She charged into the living room and shouted to the musicians to be quiet.

The band was blasting away with such enthusiasm that Marilyn had to yell three times to make her point. She made it, however. The musicians stopped playing.

Marilyn turned to face her guests. "My father . . . my father wasn't feeling well earlier this afternoon," she said. "Now he's . . . well, I don't know where he is. We can't find him. Has anybody here seen him? If he came down the stairs, somebody might have noticed."

There was murmuring and rustling. People glanced at one another. Several of the men shrugged. Jupe saw a few smiles and more than one knowing look. No one spoke up, however. No one had seen Jeremy Pilcher.

A squad car pulled into the driveway. Two police officers got out and came to the front door, where Pete admitted them. Marilyn and Sanchez led the policemen to the den across the hall.

The moment the door closed on them there was excited whispering among the guests. Then a stout elderly man with a red face said loudly, "Well!"

"Harold, whatever you plan to say, don't say it," cautioned the woman next to him.

"Don't say what?" Harold demanded. He took out a cigar. "Don't say maybe someone got to the old pirate at last?"

"Shush!" said the woman. "And if you're going to smoke, do it outside. Whew!" She made violent fanning motions with her handbag.

A sandy-haired man smiled at the woman. "Do you doubt that Jeremy Pilcher is a pirate?" he asked. His voice was mocking. "Or is it just that you don't like to admit it while you're enjoying his hospitality?"

"Watch it, Durham," said a man whose eyes glinted behind rimless glasses. "You're his lawyer, remember?"

"How could I forget?" said the lawyer. "My star client. What's with you, Ariago? You been hit with a sudden attack of loyalty? Or are you just covering something up?"

There was a hint of slurring in the lawyer's speech. Jupe wondered if he had had too much to drink.

"Meaning what exactly?" demanded Ariago.

"Oh, just that you wouldn't really bleed if something happened to Pilcher, would you? And isn't it likely that something has? Just consider his track record."

Several people gasped. Several tried to keep talking and yet go on listening to the conversation between the two men. Jim Westerbrook's mother dabbed at her temples with a lace hanky and said, "Oh dear, Jim, it *is* warm in here. Perhaps we should just step out into the garden for a few minutes."

Westerbrook seemed not to hear her, and Harry Burnside smiled rather maliciously. By this time the guests had consumed most of Burnside's buffet, and the young caterer was free to hover in the doorway and watch the excitement.

"When you were head of operations for South's Specialty Stores, you handled negotiations with the contractor who built the new branch in Pomona," said Durham. "What a nice spot to be in if you need extra cash. I understand that contractors are very generous with people who don't look too closely at the figures."

"That's a filthy lie!" shouted Ariago. "Why would you even *think* that—unless it's the sort of thing *you* would do? Is it, Durham?"

Durham was still. Ariago smiled nastily. "Pilcher has your number, Durham. You've been doing some quick deals on the stock market, haven't you? Pilcher says you're probably using money that's supposed to be held in trust for your clients."

"Shut up!" ordered Durham.

"Did Pilcher accuse you?" Ariago demanded. "Are you mad enough at him to . . . to—"

Ariago stopped abruptly. He looked around, suddenly aware that he and Durham were making a horrible scene and that everyone there could hear the accusations they hurled at each other.

The man with the cigar looked at his watch. "I had no idea it was so late," he said loudly. It was plain to see that even he had had enough. "Do you suppose the police will be with Marilyn much longer? We really have to go."

It was like a signal. The older guests started shaking hands and saying good-bye. Jupe overheard two men making a lunch date. Marilyn's young friends were not so formal. They simply drifted out through the long windows to the garden and walked away.

The party was over. When most of the guests had gone, Harry Burnside and his crew began to clear the buffet table. The husky dishwasher stripped the rose-colored tablecloths from the tables in the garden and carried them to a large hamper on wheels in the back hall. The bartender stowed his bottles in cartons.

Jupiter, Pete, and Bob helped fold up chairs and tables and carry them out to Burnside's truck, where the dishwasher loaded them in beside the hamper of linens.

They were still packing up when Marilyn and the policemen came out of the den. Marilyn pointed to the stairs. The officers went up, accompanied by Sanchez. Marilyn came across the hall to the living room.

Jim Westerbrook lingered, looking as if he wanted to be someplace else. "Are you all right?" he asked Marilyn.

"I—I suppose so," she said. "I—I just don't know what to think. I don't know whether to be afraid or what. My father could have set this up. I mean, he's so devious, and he didn't really want to give me this party. He just did it to keep me quiet. He might walk in here any minute and make a big joke about how he scared the wits out of me. Only suppose he doesn't. Suppose he's really in trouble."

"What do the cops say?" asked Westerbrook.

"They say they'll investigate. They say he hasn't been gone long. They asked if he's eccentric. Ha! Is he ever! They asked if he has any enemies. My father! Boy, does he have enemies! They asked me for names. I could have given them the Los Angeles phone directory."

"Aw, come on," said Westerbrook. "It can't be that bad."

Westerbrook's mother approached the

pair. She wore the smile of a woman determined to do the correct thing. "My dear!"
she said to Marilyn. "If there's anything we
can do, please call us at the motel."

"Thank you," said Marilyn.

Mrs. Westerbrook pulled on her gloves. "It
was a lovely party," she said. Then, realizing
that this was not quite accurate, she added,
"Lovely, until your . . . well, my dear, try not
to worry. Come along, Jim. We must let this
girl get some rest."

"I'll call you," promised Westerbrook, and
he and his mother left.

"Yep," said Marilyn under her breath. "I
just bet you'll call."

She looked around at Jupe. "Well?" she
said. "Something you want?"

"Ah . . . Miss Pilcher—Marilyn—I'm sorry," said Jupiter.

"Sure," she said. "Everybody's sorry.
What good does sorry do?"

Jupe felt that this was the moment he had
been waiting for. He had the business card of
The Three Investigators ready in his pocket.
He handed it to Marilyn, then gestured toward Pete and Bob, who hovered in the
doorway.

"We've solved some difficult cases," he
said. "We'd like a chance to help you if we
can." She glanced at the card. It said:

THE THREE INVESTIGATORS
"We Investigate Anything"
? ? ?

First Investigator .... Jupiter Jones
Second Investigator............ Peter Crenshaw
Records and Research............ Bob Andrews

Marilyn laughed. "The Three Investigators! Private detectives? You're kidding!"

She looked from Jupe to Pete and Bob. "Okay, well thanks, I guess," she said. "Only if I want a private eye, I'll get one—and he won't be any kid amateur. He'll be a pro."

Jupe nodded, only a little discouraged. Adults rarely took The Three Investigators seriously—at first. At least Marilyn tucked the card into the drawer of a lamp table instead of dropping it in the trash.

The boys left. They rode with Harry Burnside as far as his catering shop in Rocky Beach, where they helped him carry his gear inside. Then the dishwasher drove on with the truck to return the chairs and tables to the rental firm and to drop off the linens at the laundry. The boys got on their bikes and pedaled home.

After dinner Pete had to attend a birthday celebration for his grandfather, but Jupe and Bob were free to meet at The Jones Salvage Yard. The yard was owned and operated by

Jupe's Aunt Mathilda and Uncle Titus Jones. It was known all over southern California because of the many unusual items that could be found there. One of these was an old mobile home trailer that had once been in an accident. It had been displayed in a far corner of the yard until it became obvious that no one would buy it. Then Aunt Mathilda had given it to Jupe to use for a clubhouse.

A clubhouse was not what Jupe wanted. He and Bob and Pete had formed The Three Investigators detective agency, and they made the trailer into their headquarters. Fearful that Aunt Mathilda might change her mind and sell it out from under them, the boys piled salvage around the trailer so that she would not be reminded of it. They installed a telephone, which they paid for with money they earned from helping in the yard. They also set up a small crime lab in the trailer and a photographic darkroom.

When Bob arrived at the junkyard that evening, he dropped his bike in Jupe's outdoor workshop, then went directly to the trailer to review the events of the afternoon with Jupe.

"So what do you think?" asked Bob. "Is Mr. Pilcher crazy, or what?"

"He is certainly eccentric. Also, he may be

very cruel." Jupiter spoke in the deliberate way he had when he was trying to puzzle out the answer to something. "What could be more heartless than to disappear like that and upset his daughter?"

Jupe began to doodle on a pad. "His guests were an odd group," he observed. "I don't think anyone there liked him. I have the feeling they were all employees or business associates who felt they had to come. That argument between the lawyer and the other man was . . . well, it was—"

"Awful!" Bob finished the sentence for him. "Marilyn's school friends seemed fairly normal, which is kind of surprising. She's got to have the meanest mouth on campus."

The telephone rang.

Jupe picked up the phone and said, "Yes?"

Bob heard the phone make excited noises. "Ah!" said Jupe. "I see."

The telephone made some more noises.

"Very well," said Jupe.

He hung up. "That was Marilyn Pilcher," he said. "She's received a ransom note. She wants us there right away!"

5
ATTACK!

In fifteen minutes Jupe and Bob were ringing the doorbell at the Pilcher house.

Marilyn Pilcher opened the door. She still had on the blue dress she had worn at the party, but now it looked mussed. She had kicked off her high-heeled shoes.

"You got a ransom note?" said Jupe.

Marilyn handed Jupe a single sheet of paper. He read aloud: " 'Father comes back only in exchange for bishop's book. Do not call police. Act fast. Delay dangerous.' "

The word *bishop's* was penciled in huge, smudgy letters. All the other words had been cut from newspaper headlines.

"I suppose bishops don't get into the newspapers that often," said Marilyn. "The kidnapper couldn't find that word, so he had to print it himself. There wasn't an envelope. Just the note. Somebody shoved it under the back door and rang the bell and ran."

"And you're sure now it was a kidnapping?" said Jupe. "This afternoon you seemed to think your father had staged his disappearance."

"He isn't that spry," she told him. "He wouldn't be able to ring the doorbell and run. The best he can manage these days is a fast hobble. So I guess it *is* really a kidnapping, and now I have to find a bishop's book. I haven't the foggiest notion which book it might be. There must be at least eight million books in this house. So that's where you guys come in. You help me go through them and sort out whatever looks possible."

Jupe held up the ransom note. "The police should be told about this," he said. "Have you called them?"

"I have not, and you'd better not tell them either. The guy says not to, and I can't take the risk. Even if Dad isn't Father of the Year, I don't want anything to happen to him. Besides, I'll be flat broke and out of here if anything does happen. He has a clause in his will that if he dies or disappears and there's anything suspicious about it, I don't inherit a penny. Even if I'm never accused of any crime, I've had it!"

"Oh," said Jupe.

"Don't act so shocked," said Marilyn. "Dad

just likes to stack the odds in his favor. Doesn't everyone? Now, come on. Let's get busy."

She turned away and started up the stairs. The boys followed, astounded by what she had told them.

A vacuum cleaner sat in the upper hall. Marilyn had tried to get rid of the feathers from the torn pillow, but bits of white still clung to every surface. The boys ignored this and soon were working their way methodically through the bookcases in Jeremy Pilcher's bedroom. They found books on birds and books on philosophy, chemistry texts and science fiction. There were dictionaries and books on gemstones and a set of Dickens in flaking leather bindings.

"Here's something," said Jupe. He held up a dusty paperback copy of a book titled *The Bishop Murder Case*. It was a mystery by S. S. Van Dine.

Marilyn took it and flipped through the yellowing pages. "Somehow I don't think anybody would commit a crime to get their hands on this," she said. "We can try it on the kidnapper, but let's keep looking."

Bob sneezed and went on taking books from the dusty shelves, glancing at them, then putting them back. "Your dad reads a lot, doesn't he?" he said.

"Not really," Marilyn admitted. "He just buys books. He says he'll read them someday when he has more time. Meanwhile, he buys more and more, and he puts them on the shelves and there they stay. He likes owning them. It makes him feel like he knows what's in them, and once he buys a book he never gives it away. He never gives anything away."

She turned to the big bureau. "Now let's see what's in here," she murmured, and she opened one of the drawers. There were socks and a muffler and a jumble of papers. She took the papers out and shuffled through them. "Newspaper clippings," she said. "A prescription that never got filled. Some travel brochures."

She threw the papers down on the bureau. "It would help to know what we're looking for," she said. "I can't believe it's that old murder mystery."

"How about this one?" Bob held up a book titled *The Day Lincoln Was Shot*. The author was Jim Bishop.

"Unlikely, but hold it out," said Jupe.

"Maybe it's a rare first edition," said Marilyn. "Or something not even published—a manuscript. Some notes on scientific experiments? Or the logbook of somebody with terrible secrets in his past, like the commandant of a concentration camp? Something like that."

"We'll check everything," said Jupe.

The boys finished searching the room's bookcases and started to take cartons and folders down from the old collector's closet shelves. They found canceled checks tied up into packets. They found old telephone bills and postcards from far-off places like Gibraltar and Cairo. None of the postcards had been written on and mailed. Evidently they were just souvenirs.

"Dad went to sea when he was younger," Marilyn explained. "Before he became ... well, I guess a captain of industry is what you'd call him. On Wall Street they call him a pirate. Maybe he is. You can't start from nothing, the way he did, and wind up owning a shipping line and some department stores and a paper mill and two or three banks without being sharper than the next guy."

Or maybe crookeder, thought Jupe.

The telephone rang suddenly. Marilyn jumped. When she answered it, she said nothing for a moment, then cried, "I'm trying! Listen, I have something called *The Bishop Murder Case*, and a book by a guy named Jim Bishop and—"

She stopped and frowned, then said, "But I'm not trying to string you along. Listen, I

don't know what I'm looking for and . . . and
. . . wait! Listen!"

She stopped, held the phone out, and
glared at it.

"The kidnapper?" said Jupe.

"Yes. He thinks I'm making fun of him. He
doesn't want any old murder story. He wants
the bishop's book, and he hung up without
telling me any more about it."

"Could you tell anything from the voice?"
asked Bob.

She shook her head. "Hoarse," she said.
"Either the guy has a cold or he was talking
through a handkerchief to disguise his voice.
He has an accent of some kind, but that
could be a put-on."

She turned away to continue her search of
the bureau. By the time she opened the last
drawer and the boys had taken down the last
box from the closet shelves, they were all
weary. And Marilyn was hungry.

"I didn't have dinner and there's not much
in the refrigerator," she said. "Dad picked up
the tab for the food for this party, so you can
bet he made Burnside figure it really close.
Want to share a pizza?"

"Great," said Bob. "No anchovies though,
huh?"

"Extra cheese," requested Jupiter. "And a
diet cola."

"Okay. One of you guys want to come with me and help carry?"

Bob went with Marilyn, and Jupe stayed behind to continue the search. He started to go to the next bedroom, but on his way he saw the door to the attic. He had been up there that afternoon, when he and his friends were looking for Pilcher. It was not as jumbled as the unused bedrooms on the second floor. Also, it wouldn't be used as much as the bedrooms. It would be an ideal place to stash a treasure.

Jupe opened the door, flipped the light switch at the foot of the stairs, and started up.

There were trunks shoved back in the corners. There were also boxes and bookcases, but not an overwhelming number of them. Jupe went to the first set of shelves and pulled out a slim volume. It was titled *The Secret of Typewriting Speed*. It was dated 1917.

He was putting the book back on the shelf when he heard the house door close down below.

"Bob?" he called. "That you?"

There was no answer. Jupe turned from the shelf and listened, suddenly aware that it couldn't be Bob and Marilyn. Not yet. They hadn't had time to get the pizza.

But someone had come into the old collector's house.

Jupe did not call out again. He did not stir. The attic door was open, and he could hear footsteps. Someone was coming up to the second floor.

Clothing rustled. Now the intruder was at the foot of the attic stairs. Jupe heard rasping breathing.

Who was it? And did he know Jupe was there? Had he heard Jupe call out when the front door opened?

A switch clicked. The attic light went out.

The sudden darkness was so intense that it pressed in on Jupe. He felt smothered.

The prowler was coming up the attic stairs!

Jupe stepped away from the bookcase. Hide! He had to hide! He would get back in a corner, out of the way.

The footsteps were at the top of the stairs now. Jupe began to duck behind a bookcase, but he was caught suddenly in a beam of brightness. The intruder had a flashlight!

Jupe tried to dodge away, but the light followed him. The intruder came on across the attic. Jupe could see nothing but the blinding stab of light. He couldn't escape! He couldn't hide!

He lunged toward the flashlight and struck

out at it. There was a surprised gasp and a grunt of pain as one of Jupe's elbows landed on the prowler's arm. The light clattered to the floor and bounced away. Glass shattered and the attic went dark.

Now they were even. And now it began—a perilous groping in the dark as the intruder tried to get his hands on Jupe. Jupe retreated, stumbling backward, feeling his way through total blackness.

There was a touch on Jupe's shoulder, and Jupe threw himself to the side. But the assailant followed, clutching, trying to seize Jupe's arm.

Jupe doubled his fists and struck out, but he missed. Then there was a shove. Jupe stumbled and went down.

Downstairs, the house door banged open. "Jupe?" It was Bob calling. "Come and get it!"

A voice muttered something Jupe did not understand. The attacker floundered through the blackness to the attic stairs and thundered down and away.

Jupe scrambled up and made for the stairs. He almost fell as he raced down after the intruder. When he reached the second floor he heard his quarry on the back stairs.

Bob called again. "Hey, what's up? Jupe?"

Jupe dashed down to the kitchen just in

time to hear the back door slam. By the time he got the door open again, the stranger had crossed the yard and disappeared down the alley.

6

FOOTSTEPS IN THE NIGHT

Marilyn called the police. They came and took a report on the intruder. They searched the shrubbery around the house. They looked into the garage in back. Then they told Marilyn to call 911 if the prowler returned.

The police also asked if her father had been heard from, and they reassured her that most missing persons showed up on their own. Marilyn said nothing to the officers about a ransom note. She stood in the doorway and watched the squad car drive off, then she sighed. "Who *was* that prowler? An ordinary burglar? The kidnapper? This is getting really confusing."

"I'd vote for the kidnapper," said Bob. "Maybe he got impatient waiting for the bishop's book."

"Perhaps," said Jupe. "Though we have a better chance of finding the book than an

intruder does. But it does suggest that someone has been watching the house."

Marilyn looked around fearfully. "I think
I'll go to my mother's for the night," she said.
"This place is too creepy."

"Does your mother live near here?" asked
Jupe.

"In Santa Monica," said Marilyn. "She
and Dad are divorced. Yes, that's what
I'll do. I'll go there. Except . . . maybe I
shouldn't. If the kidnapper calls again, I
should be here to take the call. Maybe I'll
phone Ray Sanchez and ask him to come
over. He's Dad's secretary, so I guess he'd do
it. I could offer him some overtime."

"Couldn't your fiancé and his mother come
over?" asked Jupe.

"They could—if they hadn't called earlier
to say there was a family emergency and
they were flying home to Boston tonight."
Marilyn snorted. "I bet the emergency was
getting away from the Pilchers."

"Bob and I could stay here for the night,"
Jupe suggested.

The young woman blinked, and for a second she seemed to struggle with herself, as if
she didn't want to appear pleased at the
idea. But finally she said, "Well, sure! I'm
your client, so why shouldn't you be bodyguards? Will your folks let you stay?"

"Probably," said Jupe. "They're pretty good about things like this."

Jupe was right. He and Bob telephoned their homes and had little trouble getting permission to spend the night at the Pilcher house so that Marilyn wouldn't be alone. After they phoned, Bob reheated the pizza he and Marilyn had brought. They ate, then renewed their search for the bishop's book. They turned out the shelves in the cluttered rooms on the second floor and found more books and more papers and more relics of the days when Pilcher was a seaman voyaging to far-off lands.

"Your dad must have been kind of adventurous when he was younger," said Bob when he came upon an ivory elephant that Marilyn told him was from India. "He must have had a ball, going to sea and everything."

"He could afford to be adventurous then," said Marilyn gloomily. "When he was younger he didn't have anything to lose, so he just went where he wanted. But then he somehow got enough together to buy the Comet Steamship Line. It wasn't much—just a couple of rusty freighters that sailed out of Houston to ports in the Caribbean. They were tramp steamers that went wherever they were needed. Dad was smart, and he made enough with those two old scows to have a third ship built. That one made even more money. Then Dad bought a little bank up in Visalia, and he did some deals on the stock market.

"Mom says it was after he got into the stock market that he really got excited about making money. She says it was like watching someone turn into a compulsive gambler. I— I don't think Mom understands him."

"And you do?" said Bob.

She shrugged. "I think I do, as much as anybody. I just wish he wasn't such a hoarder. Not that he's that way in business. In business you've got to know when to let go. That's one of the things Dad taught me. You have to be sharp, because if you're not, the turkeys will get you down.

"I was about five when he and Mom got the divorce. Most of the time I live with my mom when I'm not in school. Lately, though, I've been spending more time with Dad. I wouldn't want him to forget he has a daughter."

It was late when they finished searching the rooms on the second floor. Marilyn said good night and disappeared into her bedroom. Bob and Jupe decided to take turns keeping watch in the upper hall. They were close enough to Marilyn to hear her if something frightened her during the night. Also, they could see both the front and back stairs. No one could creep up on them and surprise them.

Bob took the first shift. He got an armchair from one of the bedrooms and settled himself with a cola in his hand.

Jupe took a blanket from the linen closet and stretched out on a bed in one of the unused rooms, thinking he probably wouldn't sleep a wink after the excitement of the day.

The next thing he knew, Bob was shaking him. "It's three A.M.," said Bob. "I'm beat. Your turn to watch."

Jupe crawled out from under the blanket. Bob crawled in. "Mmmm!" said Bob. "Thanks for warming it up for me."

"You aren't welcome," said Jupe grumpily. He went out to the post in the hall, feeling chilled and depressed, and sat down in the chair. He decided that three A.M. had to be the lowest hour of the day. Compared with three A.M., midnight was cheery.

How long would it be before daybreak, he wondered.

As this thought came, something moved over his head. He looked up, not breathing, listening.

Nothing! Dead silence. The dreary old house was getting on his nerves. He was imagining things.

But then it came again. It was a mere whisper of movement, as if someone walked across the attic floor on bare feet—someone small and light.

But no one could be up there!

Jupe stood up and went slowly, silently, to the attic door. Slowly, silently, he turned the doorknob and eased the door open.

He looked up into total darkness, and he smelled the chill dead smell of the unused space above.

Someone was there. Someone was at the top of the stairs. He couldn't see anything, but he could hear the faintest rustle of clothing, the sigh as a breath was expelled. And he knew that the unseen one could look down over the stair rail and watch him.

For a second Jupe bitterly regretted not turning out the hall light before he opened the door. If the stalker in the darkness had a weapon, Jupe would make a first-rate target.

Was it the intruder who had attacked him earlier? If it was, why had he come back? And how had he gotten inside? What was he doing in the attic?

Jupe stepped back and eased the attic door shut.

"What is it?" whispered someone close behind Jupe.

Jupe jumped as though he had been shot.

"Hey, it's only me."

Bob was there looking tousled, his shoes off. He gestured toward the ceiling. "Somebody's walking around up there," he said. He still spoke in a whisper.

"You heard it too?"

A board creaked above them. The intruder had left the stairwell. He was going toward the front of the house.

"You fell asleep," Jupe accused his pal. "That guy came in and walked right past you, and you were sound asleep and didn't see him!"

"No way!" Bob declared. "Not for a second. I had to get up a couple of times and walk around to keep awake, but I kept awake!"

Jupe scowled at the ceiling. "Well, however he got in, he certainly knows he's not alone. He knows we're here, and he knows that we know he's here, and so—"

Jupe yanked open the attic door and called out. "Hey! Who's there?"

No one answered, but the unseen one stopped walking.

Jupe called again.

Still there was no answer.

Jupe flicked on the attic light.

"You're not going up there!" cried Bob. "Suppose the guy's got a gun?"

"He'd have shot me by now if he was going to shoot me," said Jupe. He sounded confident—more confident than he really felt.

He went up the stairs in a rush. He wanted to get to the top before the person who lurked in the attic could get back to the stairwell.

He reached the top unharmed, but no one was there! The attic was empty. Jupe saw bookcases and trunks and boxes, and that was all.

He stood still and listened.

Not a sound.

He went back to the stairs and looked down. Bob was looking up at him.

"Nothing," said Jupe. "We—we must be sharing some kind of . . . hallucination!"

"I don't believe that!" said Bob.

"There's nobody here," insisted Jupe. "Unless . . . unless there's some way to get in and out of here without coming down the stairs! That's it! This is an old house. There could be a hidden passageway—something nobody knows about!"

Marilyn appeared behind Bob in the hall. She was wearing a quilted robe and a grumpy expression. "What's the matter with you two?" she demanded. "Jupe, what are you doing up there?"

"Marilyn, could there be a secret passageway in this house? Have you ever heard of one? Even a rumor of one?"

"No." She shook her head.

Jupe searched. He looked behind boxes and trunks. He moved things that stood near the chimney, thinking a door might be concealed next to the bricks. He got a flashlight from the kitchen, then crawled around on his hands and knees to examine the open area between the end of the floorboards and the place where the roof slanted down to meet the joists. Here for a foot or two, he could see the lath and plaster of the bedroom ceilings. He sent a beam of light into the space under the floorboards. But he saw nothing except the grime that had collected over the years, plus some odds and ends that people had dropped and then forgotten. He recovered an old golf ball, an empty cola bottle, and a few bits of crumpled paper.

When he was satisfied that he had examined every inch of the attic, Jupe went down to the hall where Marilyn and Bob waited.

"Weird!" said Bob.

"You guys are hearing things!" Marilyn accused.

She went back to her room and closed the door.

Bob went for his blanket, wrapped it

around himself, and settled down on the floor next to the armchair.

"You aren't going back to bed?" said Jupe. "It's my watch, you know."

"I don't think I want to be by myself," Bob confessed. "I'll stay here and keep you company."

So the two Investigators spent the remaining hours before daylight watching the staircases, watching the ceiling, and listening— always listening.

Once Bob thought he heard the stealthy footsteps again, but the sound was so soft he couldn't be sure.

At last a thin gray light began to show at the windows. Soon the sun would be up. The long, dreary watch was over.

But Jupe stiffened. He heard a key rattle in a lock! Downstairs! The kitchen door! Someone was at the kitchen door. Someone who had a key.

Jupe was up and out of his chair. A weapon! He mustn't go down there without a weapon!

Bob flung his blanket aside.

Jupe touched his lips, signaling silence, and seized a tarnished brass plate that hung on the wall near the attic stairs. It was the only thing he could grab. It would be a clumsy weapon, but it would have to do.

He started down the back stairs with Bob behind him.

At the bottom of the stairs the two stared across the kitchen. The upper half of the kitchen door was glass, but a shade had been drawn to cover it. There was no way to tell who was there.

Jupe went forward, his brass plate held ready.

The rattling stopped. The door swung in.

Jupe lifted the plate, ready to strike!

7
THE SECRET FILES

"Saints preserve us!"

A gray-haired woman shrank away from Jupe. She threw her arm up to protect her face.

Jupe was paralyzed with surprise. For a second he froze, his brass plate still held ready. Then he realized that the gray-haired little woman with the string shopping bag couldn't possibly be a menace. "I'm very sorry," he said. He lowered the brass plate.

"Police!" shouted the woman. "Help!" She turned and fled toward the alley.

"No, wait!" yelled Jupe. "Please! Just a minute!"

Marilyn Pilcher tumbled downstairs in her bathrobe and her bare feet. "Mrs. McCarthy, wait!" she cried.

She raced past Jupe and caught the woman when she was halfway down the alley. "Wait! It's only Jupe and Bob. They're okay, honest."

The woman let herself be coaxed back to the kitchen. "Bob, Jupe, this is Mrs. Mc-Carthy, my father's housekeeper," said Marilyn. "Mrs. Mac, Jupe and Bob are my bodyguards."

Mrs. McCarthy glared at the boys. She was breathing hard. Jupe guessed that her sprint across the backyard was her most athletic feat in years.

"Bodyguards, is it?" she said at last. "Since when are you such a treasure that you need a bodyguard? And where's your father? He's bodyguard enough for anyone, I'm thinkin'. The old heathen would scare off the devil himself if Old Nick took it into his head to come round."

"Dad's not here," said Marilyn. "He disappeared. Yesterday. He was kidnapped."

"Kidnapped? You don't mean it!"

Marilyn insisted that she did mean it. She told about the mysterious disappearance, and she showed Mrs. McCarthy the ransom note. "The boys are helping me," she explained. "We're looking for the bishop's book, whatever that is. Have you ever heard Dad talk about a bishop's book?"

"I have not," said the housekeeper. "Your

father and the clergy were not well acquaint-
ed, as you know. And are you sure it's someone got in and got him and then sent that
note? You know he doesn't like that poor
pale briggle you've taken it into your head to
marry, no more than I do. Not much *to* that
one, if you ask me. And it was foolish of your
father to give in to you about that party. But
you *would* have it, wouldn't you? And on a
Sunday, when I don't work. And now your
father might be trying to scare you so you'd
forget the idea of a weddin'."

"That isn't it," said Marilyn. "At least I
don't think that's it. I can't take a chance,
can I? The kidnapper might do something
awful to him."

Mrs. McCarthy shook her head. "A bad
business," she said. She dived into her string
bag and took out an apron. She put it on and
started to fix breakfast, all the time keeping
up a steady stream of talk.

"It's this house," she said. "It's an unlucky
house. Always has been. Built by a man
named Harrison Reeves, long ago. I heard
the story from my neighbor Dolly Jessup.
Reeves was a rich man, but the day the house
was finished he lost everything. The stock
market crashed—you know, in 1929. Reeves
never lived here, and the house stood empty

for years. Then, just after I moved here from New York, a family named Whitney bought the place. I remember them. He was a big strappin' fellow. He fell on the stairs before the year was out and broke his hip, and he never walked right again.

"After the Whitneys there was Miss Jensen. An old maid with more money than was good for her, and fond of it, she was. She had a niece come to live with her. I remember the niece—a nice little thing, but sad. Miss Jensen was so stern with her. She had to come right home after school and help with getting the dinner. Miss Jensen claimed that would build character. Saved the old biddy from hiring servants is what I'm thinkin'. A shame it was, when all the other young ones in the neighborhood were out playing up and down the street.

"When the girl was about fourteen there was trouble about a pin Miss Jensen couldn't find. She said the girl must have taken it, and she sent the girl back to her parents in disgrace. I heard the girl ran off with some scoundrel some years after. He left her eventually. She was living in San Francisco, last I heard, working in a market."

Mrs. McCarthy put eggs and toast and bacon in front of Marilyn and the boys, then sat down herself to have a cup of coffee.

"Have you ever heard that the house is haunted?" asked Jupiter. "With all that trouble, weren't there ever rumors?"

"Well, people do talk," said the housekeeper. "But people always talk about old houses. I don't know. I've never seen anything, but the place *is* unlucky. And sometimes, when the weather's gray, I get a feeling that there's something . . . something that watches me. It's—it's nothing I can put a name to, but I'd not stay here at night, I'll tell you that!"

"Oh, nonsense!" said Marilyn.

"Have you ever heard anything walking around in the attic?" asked Bob.

"In the attic? No. I've never heard anything at all—not in the attic or anywhere else. It's just that I'm . . . I feel as if something's here somewhere."

She sipped her coffee and looked gloomy.

The boys let the subject drop. Mrs. McCarthy couldn't help them. But it seemed clear that last night's creepy incident was something new in the house.

When breakfast was over, the boys took themselves off to The Jones Salvage Yard, where they reported to Aunt Mathilda.

Jupiter expected his aunt to be curious about the Pilchers, but that day Aunt Ma-

thilda had no time for curiosity. An old brick
building in Pasadena was being demolished,
and Uncle Titus had just brought in a load of
used bricks from the site. Aunt Mathilda
directed the boys to clean the bricks, knocking off any bits of mortar that clung to them.
Pete joined Bob and Jupe shortly before
eleven and helped them pile the clean bricks
in a neat heap near some ancient timbers.

When they finished with the bricks, the
boys went across the street to the Jones
house. They washed up and then made sand-
wiches, which they carried to Jupe's workshop.

The workshop was in a corner of the salvage yard well away from the office and the
front gate. It was sheltered by an overhang
that ran around the inside of the fence. Jupe
had his workbench there and a small print-
ing press that he had repaired when it came
into the yard as junk.

The Three Investigators were munching
away when a light over the workbench began
to flash, signaling that the telephone in
Headquarters was ringing. Jupe quickly
pulled aside a grating that appeared to be
leaning against the bottom of the workbench.
Behind the grating was the open end of a
huge galvanized iron pipe. This was Tunnel

Two, one of the secret passages that the boys could use to enter their headquarters unobserved.

Jupe was a pudgy boy, not built for negotiating tight places. But he could get through the pipe in nothing flat when there was a call for The Three Investigators. He bent double now, ducked into the pipe, and scrambled through so quickly that the phone was only on its fifth ring when he pushed at the wooden trap door at the far end of Tunnel Two. It swung up to let him into Headquarters.

He picked up the telephone as Bob and Pete came into the mobile home trailer behind him. The call was from Raymond Sanchez, Jeremy Pilcher's secretary.

"Marilyn asked me to call you," Sanchez said. "We've been looking for that mysterious book all morning, and we can't find anything. Marilyn thinks that if I boot up her father's computer so we can look at his files, we may learn something. Only we don't know the password that will get us into his files.

"Marilyn wants you to come. Maybe you can guess what the old goat—er, what Mr. Pilcher would have used for a password."

Jupe turned to Bob and Pete and repeated

Ray's message. "What do you say? Want to go over to Marilyn's and see if we can guess the password?"

"Yeah," said Pete. "Okay, I guess."

Bob nodded.

"We'll be right there," Jupe told Sanchez. He hung up. "Sounds like our client has accepted us," he said.

"I'm not sure I've accepted her," said Pete. "She can be almost as prickly as her old man."

But Pete followed Jupe and Bob out of Headquarters. In minutes the Three Investigators were ringing the bell at the Pilcher house. Mrs. McCarthy opened the door for them. She had a spray bottle of window cleaner in one hand and a roll of paper towels tucked under the other arm. "Just going to get a few things cleaned while the old grump is out of the way," she said cheerfully. "When he's around, I can't do it. You boys come along. Marilyn and Ray are in the computer room."

They went up the stairs behind Mrs. McCarthy. At the top she gestured them forward, then vanished into one of the cluttered bedrooms.

In the computer room Ray Sanchez was seated in front of the smaller of the two computers. Keys clicked under his fingers. The computer beeped.

Marilyn stood behind Sanchez and watched the monitor.

"This is Dad's private computer," she told the boys. "The big one is part of the system that's been installed in Dad's office downtown, but this smaller one isn't part of any system. It doesn't have a modem, so nobody from outside can get into the memory. If we can figure out the password, we can look at Dad's private files. We might find that 'bishop's book' is just a code name for something else."

Sanchez shook his head. "All this stuff about a book is bilge," he said. "I'll bet somebody with a grudge against Pilcher set up the kidnapping. Lots of people would be ahead if Pilcher disappeared. Or maybe he decided he'd just drop out of sight for a while. He's a weird guy. He could have his reasons."

"He's your boss," Marilyn snapped. "Have some respect!"

"Sorry," said Sanchez. He turned back to the keyboard. "Mr. Pilcher collects information on his associates," he told the boys. "He checks out backgrounds and private lives and everything. I should know. Sometimes the background check means there's a private investigator involved. I took care of paying some P.I.s' bills, but I never got to see their final reports. I know some of the stuff Pilcher gets is too hot to go into the company files downtown. Maybe he puts it in this machine. But a bishop's book? He didn't know any bishops."

"A code name," insisted Marilyn. "It could be a code name."

"Well, it isn't the password, we know that," said Sanchez. "I tried that and got zilch."

He thought for a minute, then typed in the word HUSTLER.

"Hustler?" said Pete.

"You know about hustlers, don't you? They pretend they don't know how to play a game, and they lure unsuspecting marks into playing with them. Then—whap! They win, and win big! That's the kind of setup Mr. Pilcher likes. It's the reason he sometimes employs people who have shady backgrounds. He's more comfortable when he can hold things over people."

"That's only smart, isn't it?" said Marilyn Pilcher.

No one answered her.

The computer beeped, and a message appeared on the monitor: INCORRECT PASSWORD. TRY AGAIN.

CON ARTIST typed Sanchez.

Again the machine beeped and the message INCORRECT PASSWORD appeared.

"You really are a—a rat!" cried Marilyn.

"We can stop anytime," said Sanchez coolly. "It was your idea!"

"We can't stop!" Marilyn insisted. "We have to know. But you needn't be so insulting. You know business is a game to him. He's like a high-pressure football coach. Would you like it better if he said a lot of corny stuff about always playing fair? No! You'd think he was a wimp, and you'd be right. Winning! That's what counts, and you know it!"

Jupe had been watching quietly, his eyes almost sleepy. Now he suddenly came to attention. "A game," he said. "Your dad talked about business as a game? Could that be a clue to the password?"

Sanchez typed in the word GAME. The machine beeped its discouraging beep.

"Try different games," suggested Bob. "Try 'football,' for a start."

"Football" was not the answer. Neither was "baseball," "basketball," or "hockey."

"My father doesn't really care for sports,"

said Marilyn. "Try another direction."

Sanchez keyed in MONOPOLY. "That's a game Mr. Pilcher would like," he said.

"Monopoly" was not the password.

"Try 'poker,' " said Pete.

Sanchez ran through "poker," "gin rummy," "pinochle," and "blackjack."

"Card names," said Jupe. "Try 'ace' or 'king.' "

Sanchez tried. "Ace" and "king" were not it, but when the secretary typed in JOKER, the machine beeped, and this time the beep was triumphant. A different message appeared on the screen. COME ON, LET'S PLAY! invited the computer.

"Hot dog!" crowed Pete.

Sanchez typed a command to the computer: LIST/F.

A long list of names appeared on the monitor. Pilcher had a file on Ariago, and one on Durham, the lawyer. Sanchez recognized the name of the manager of Pilcher's bank in Visalia and the names of other key employees. There was even a file for Mrs. McCarthy, the housekeeper.

And there was a file entitled "Sanchez."

"He checked up on you, too," Bob said to the secretary.

"Of course," said Sanchez. "He checks up on everybody."

But Jupe saw that there was a slick of moisture on Sanchez's face. The secretary was sweating.

Marilyn Pilcher saw it too. "What's in your file?" she demanded.

"Probably the usual stuff," said Sanchez. "You know, age, education, stuff like that."

"I want to see it." Marilyn's voice was harsh.

"Marilyn, for Pete's sake—"

"I want to see it!"

Sanchez shrugged. He pressed a key. The cursor moved to his name on the list. He pressed another key. The list vanished and SANCHEZ, RAYMOND appeared on the monitor, followed by the notation REAL NAME, LUIS ESTAVA. SON OF JORGE ESTAVA. PROBABLY TRYING TO GET SOMETHING ON ME. WILL KEEP HIM AROUND FOR A WHILE. A GOOD WORKER. IT'S FUN TO WATCH HIM SWEAT AND BUMBLE.

Sanchez jumped up and headed for the door. "I'm leaving!" he said. "I won't be back!"

8
THE MYSTERIOUS MESSAGE

"Good grief!" Marilyn put one hand to her throat. "Ray is Jorge Estava's son! Why, it could be him! Ray could be the kidnapper!"

Jupe raised an eyebrow. "He might be the instigator, but he couldn't have committed the crime himself. He was at the party the whole time, remember? But why would he want to kidnap your father? Who is Jorge Estava?"

"A man who owns . . . who owned a tire dealership in West Los Angeles. It had a good corner location. Dad wanted the corner for a high-rise office building. Estava wouldn't sell, not even when Dad upped his offer, so Dad opened a tire dealership right next door to Estava and undersold him. I mean, *really* undersold him. Estava tried to hang on, but he couldn't afford to sell at a loss, and Dad could. In six months Estava folded."

"So the guy's son gets a job here, using a fake name," concluded Bob. "He wants to get back at your father, but your father finds out who he really is. I wonder how Sanchez thought he'd get away with it once he found out that your father has everyone investigated."

"Perhaps he thought his cover story was good enough to fool an investigator," said Jupe. He sat down at the keyboard and gave the computer the command to print the complete file on Ray Sanchez. The printer clattered to life, and in half a minute the print-out was ready. Jupe read it aloud to his friends.

Sanchez had used the address and telephone number of a high school friend when he applied for the job with Jeremy Pilcher. A routine background check on Sanchez had turned up nothing suspicious, but Pilcher had a private investigator tail the young man anyway. He learned that Sanchez went to the Estava home in Ocean Park every night when he quit work. Pilcher's investigator talked to the neighbors, pretending to be from an insurance company, and he learned the truth.

"Well, Sanchez/Estava sure has a motive

for the kidnapping," said Bob. "Only—only
he doesn't seem to me like somebody who'd
get violent."

"He isn't," said Marilyn. "And this bishop's book thing—it doesn't make sense. Not
for Ray Sanchez and . . . and I don't feel
well."

She sat down in front of the larger computer and shut her eyes. "I can't believe it
was Ray. If Ray did it, he'd have found a way
to sabotage this computer. It must be someone else."

Jupe nodded. "Okay. Let's look at some
other files." He called up the file on Ted
Ariago.

The information on Ariago looked routine
at first. Ariago was a widower. He had no
children, and he lived in a town house in the
Larchmont area. Before taking the position
of manager of the Santa Monica branch of
the A. L. Becket Department Store, Ariago
had been director of operations at a non-
Pilcher enterprise—South's Specialty Stores.

The dossier on Ariago quickly became
more than routine. The man had once been
arrested and charged with attempting to
defraud an insurance company; there had
been a fire in a building Ariago owned, and
the insurance company suspected arson. The
charge was dismissed for lack of evidence.

Then, Ariago had left South's Stores amid rumors that he had taken payoffs from builders and suppliers who worked on projects for the company.

There was also a terse note at the end of the file: "Woman-chaser."

The file on Chuck Durham, Pilcher's lawyer, was almost as interesting as the one on Ariago. Durham was a gambler, addicted to horse racing, poker, and also to taking some high risks on the stock market. Pilcher suspected him of using funds that he held in trust for some minors, and had threatened to contact the bar association and ask for an investigation of his accounts. Pilcher felt the threat would "keep him in line."

The file on the man who managed Pilcher's bank in Visalia showed he had a less-than-honorable discharge from the Navy. Pilcher knew it and let the man know that he knew it.

Jupe called up file after file. One secret after another flashed on the monitor. Even Mrs. McCarthy had her fatal flaw. She was addicted to the weekly bingo games at St. Athanasius' Parish.

"I don't think this is getting us anywhere," said Marilyn Pilcher at last. "All it shows is that . . . that we had a houseful of people yesterday who hated Dad's guts. He doesn't have *any* friends. I hate that. And I hate it that he took the trouble to find out all this stuff."

She was almost in tears. For the moment she was not defending her father.

Jupe had to agree that the secret files weren't really helpful. Everyone listed had a motive for wanting Pilcher out of the way, but no one person stood out. Everyone was a suspect, and no one was.

"There's one more file," Jupe said. "We might as well see it. It's called 'Mujer/vieja.' That means 'old woman' in Spanish."

"Big deal!" said Pete. "It's probably more about Mrs. McCarthy. She's been conspiring to fix those bingo games!"

"Why would a file on Mrs. McCarthy be in Spanish?" said Jupe reasonably, and he called it up.

It was quite different from the other files. It was a letter, and it was directed to Marilyn.

START SOGAMOSO, said the computer screen. GO TO OLD WOMAN. AT SUNSET ON MIDSUMMER DAY HER SHADOW TOUCHES THE TEARS OF THE GODS. ALL FOR YOU, BUT WATCH OUT FOR NAVARRO. IS HE LEGAL? CHECK INS.

"Well, now," said Jupe. He ordered the computer to make a print-out of this cryptic message. As the print head flew across the paper, he looked hopefully at Marilyn.

She shook her head.

"It doesn't mean anything to you?" asked Jupiter.

"Not a thing."

"You're supposed to watch out for Navarro," Jupe persisted. "Do you know somebody named Navarro?"

Marilyn shrugged. "Another of Dad's charming business associates, I suppose. There was no Navarro at the party. I guess Dad missed a few deadly enemies when he made up the guest list."

The boys saw that she was crying. The tears ran down her cheeks, and she did not even try to wipe them away.

"Okay," said Jupe. "Maybe we can find a clue someplace else."

He turned away from the computer. Bob held up a small notebook that he had just found in a drawer. "An address book," he said. "Handwritten."

The boys went through the book, page by page, but there was no one named Navarro listed.

"My mom might know," said Marilyn. She had recovered somewhat from her silent fit of weeping. "Mom and Dad aren't on speaking terms now, but she might remember someone from the old days when they were together."

"Are you going to call her and ask?" Pete wanted to know.

"Ah . . . it's awkward. Right now she's mad at me too. She doesn't like my coming here to be with Dad and she doesn't like my fiancé and . . . well, never mind, I'll try her."

Marilyn picked up the telephone and dialed. When the call was answered, a voice said a lot more than hello. "She's out," explained Marilyn to the boys. "I've got her answering machine."

There was a beep from the phone.

"Mother, it's me," said Marilyn. "Listen, I think Dad may have been kidnapped. Some boys here are trying to find out for sure. Mom, if Jupiter Jones and Pete Crenshaw and Bob Andrews come to see you, would you talk to them? They want to find out about somebody named Navarro. And Soga-moso, too. If you think of anything, tell them, huh? I'll be home soon, but I can't leave until I find out about Dad. 'Bye, Mom."

She hung up. "That should do it. My mom's an okay person, really. She doesn't wish anybody bad luck—not even Dad."

The boys gathered up the print-outs Jupe had made, and Marilyn wrote down her mother's address for them. After a brief conference they decided that Pete would stay with Marilyn for the rest of the day and also that night, since Mrs. McCarthy had a husband and she planned to go home to him. Bob announced that he had some chores to do at home and volunteered to go to the Rocky Beach Library after dinner. He would search reference books for some mention of Sogamoso.

"There's no sense even looking for references to Navarro," he told Jupe. "There must be a zillion Navarros just in the Los Angeles phone book. But Sogamoso isn't a name you hear every day. It might be a lead."

"It may not be a person," Jupe pointed out. "It could be a place or even a company."

Jupiter was elected to visit Mrs. Pilcher. He said good-bye to Marilyn and his pals, and rode on down the highway to Santa Monica.

Mrs. Pilcher's home turned out to be a rambling one-story residence on a quiet street. Unlike the unkempt Pilcher mansion in Rocky Beach, it sparkled with fresh paint. The lawn was well-tended and very green. The walk leading to the house had a just-swept look.

Mrs. Pilcher answered the doorbell herself. A pleasant-looking woman with hair the color of taffy and eyes to match, she was too plump to be fashionable, but her skin was smooth and unwrinkled. She was much younger than Jeremy Pilcher.

"I suppose you're one of the boys Marilyn phoned about," said Mrs. Pilcher. "I was out when the call came. I can't give you much time. I'm expecting a . . . a guest. Come in."

She led Jupe through an entrance hall into a living room with soft-green carpeting, and furniture covered with white linen.

Mrs. Pilcher sat down in a big chair near the fireplace. "Is Marilyn all right?" she said. "Why doesn't she come home?"

"She wants to be there if the kidnapper calls," said Jupe.

"I should go over there," said Mrs. Pilcher, "but I just hate to. I hate that house. Things started going wrong for us the day we moved in there. Marilyn isn't alone, is she?"

"My friend Pete is with her," said Jupiter.

"Your friend? A boy, I suppose. Where are the police? She shouldn't be there with just a boy to protect her."

"Pete's an athlete," said Jupe. "He's faster and stronger than a lot of adults. Also, it wouldn't be in the best interests of the kidnapper to harm Marilyn, would it? He wants her to give him the bishop's book."

"Bishop's book?" Mrs. Pilcher was sitting

forward, tense and listening. Jupe had the feeling she was barely listening to him. She was tuned in to something else, something that might be happening in some far part of the house.

For a second Jupe said nothing. He listened, too. But nothing seemed to stir anywhere nearby. The house was very quiet.

"Do you know anything about a bishop's book?" Jupe asked.

She shook her head. "No. No, I don't. But I don't know a lot about what Jeremy is doing these days. We've been divorced for years. Is that why you wanted to see me? To see if I know about a book? Jeremy has tons of books. Did you look at them?"

"Yes, ma'am," said Jupiter. "We couldn't find the one the kidnapper wants. Mrs. Pilcher, do you know anyone named Navarro? Or Sogamoso?"

"Soga . . . who?"

Jupe sighed.

"I'm not being much help, am I?" said Mrs. Pilcher. "I'm sorry. If I knew, I'd tell you. What was that name again? The one that isn't Navarro?"

"Sogamoso," said Jupe.

She shook her head. "No. Sorry."

"Have you ever heard Mr. Pilcher talk of an old woman?" Jupe asked. "In Spanish it's *mujer vieja*. He could have used the Spanish phrase."

She had not. Nor could she recall Jeremy Pilcher speaking of tears of the gods. She answered in quick short phrases, and it was plain that she was anxious to have Jupe gone.

"Tears of the gods sounds poetic," she said, "but Jeremy is not a poetic person. I'm sorry. I just don't know. Have you looked aboard the *Bonnie Betsy*? Sometimes Jeremy kept things there."

"The *Bonnie Betsy*?" said Jupiter.

"Jeremy's yacht. It's named *Bonnie Betsy* after me. My name is Elizabeth. Things were a bit more cordial between us when Jeremy christened the yacht."

She stood up. The visit was over. Jupe followed her to the door, where he gave her one of The Three Investigators' business cards. "If you think of anything that might help us, call this number," he said.

She promised that she would, and Jupe went out.

Jupe rode his bike as far as the corner, then stopped to wait for a bus to go through the intersection. He glanced back toward Mrs. Pilcher's house.

A stocky figure was coming down the front walk toward the street. It was a man Jupe had seen before—a man who had been a guest at Marilyn's party.

"Ariago!" Jupe was so surprised that he spoke aloud.

Ariago had a motive for wanting Pilcher out of the way. What was he doing in Mrs. Pilcher's house?

He must have been there while Mrs. Pilcher and Jupe talked. Had he hidden someplace, listening to Jupe's conversation with Mrs. Pilcher? Jupe pictured him crouched in the kitchen, his ear to the door.

No wonder Mrs. Pilcher had been tense, had hurried Jupe on his way. She wasn't waiting for a guest—the guest was already there. A guest she wanted to hide.

Could Mrs. Pilcher and Ariago be conspirators? It seemed out of character for the pleasant-looking woman, yet it was possible. Anything was possible.

Jupe watched Ariago cross the street and get into a car that was parked some distance from the Pilcher house. He saw the brake lights go on. A gust of exhaust came from the tailpipe. In a second Ariago would drive off.

On an impulse Jupe turned his bike around. As Ariago pulled away from the curb, Jupe was a couple of hundred yards behind him, pedaling furiously.

9
THE PROWLER
RETURNS

Bob arrived at the library later than he'd hoped. He quickly decided that the telephone directories on the library shelves would be no help. There were columns and columns of listings for Navarro in the Los Angeles telephone book but not a single one for Sogamoso.

Bob sighed, spread the print-out of the computer message on the table in front of him, and scowled at it.

MARILYN—START SOGAMOSO, read the message. GO TO OLD WOMAN. AT SUNSET ON MIDSUMMER DAY HER SHADOW TOUCHES THE TEARS OF THE GODS. ALL FOR YOU, BUT WATCH OUT FOR NAVARRO. IS HE LEGAL? CHECK INS.

What now, Bob wondered. The names of Navarro and Sogamoso were the only real clues the message contained. The initials INS probably referred to the Immigration

and Naturalization Service, and Navarro
might be an illegal alien. It wasn't very
helpful to know that. Unless perhaps Pilcher
meant that his daughter was to turn Navarro
in to the INS if the man appeared. Meanwhile, the message was so obscure that it
was maddening.

And why would Jeremy Pilcher leave a
cryptic note in the memory of his computer?
Marilyn did not seem to be a computer whiz.
Pilcher couldn't have been sure she would
ever see the message.

But perhaps Pilcher hadn't had time to
make a more sensible plan. He might have
suddenly become aware that he was threatened. If the person who threatened him
knew nothing about computers, the message
could be hidden in Pilcher's machine safely
enough. But if Marilyn didn't understand a
word of it, it would do her no good either.

Bob worked part-time in this library, and
he knew its layout well. He went over to the
reference shelves where there were directories of business firms. Jeremy Pilcher was
a businessman, so there was a good chance
that Sogamoso had something to do with a
business. Bob looked for Sogamoso in
Standard & Poor's, a big book that listed
American companies. He went through the
index to *The Wall Street Journal* and to *Forbes*

magazine. He found no mention of Sogamoso. The name did not appear in any edition of *Who's Who*.

Well then, thought Bob, Sogamoso was not
a prominent person. It was not a business.
Sogamoso must be something else entirely.

The idea sent him to a Spanish-English
dictionary. When he did not find the word
there, he went doggedly on to the big atlas
on the bottom shelf in the reference section.
And there at last he found it—in the index at
the back.

Sogamoso was a town in Colombia.

"The library will close in ten minutes!"
warned a voice on the public-address system.

Frantically Bob turned to the page number
given in the index. It showed a map of the
northwest corner of South America. Colombia was there, its borders outlined in purple,
the lofty Andes Mountains depicted as white
ridges running slantwise on the page.

Bob squinted. Sogamoso. The index had
given the population of the place as a little
over 49,000. It wasn't a large city.

It turned out to be a speck in the mountains northeast of Bogotá. Why on earth
would Pilcher want Marilyn to go to this
remote place and find an old woman? And
would any old woman do? Or must it be one
particular old woman?

A brief description of Colombia appeared next to the map. "Colombia is almost unsettled," Bob read, "except in the narrow region between the coast and the western foothills of the Andes. In the wet lowlands near the coast, sugar cane and cacao are grown. In the altitudes from 3,000 to 6,500 feet Colombians grow one of the largest coffee crops in the world. Wheat and barley are raised in the mountain basins, and sheep are herded in the alpine meadows. Textiles are manufactured in the Antioquia Valley. A steel industry exists in the iron and coal area near Sogamoso, and there are also gold and emerald mines in the mountains. Most Colombians depend on income from coffee."

The overhead lights flicked. "The library will close in five minutes," said the loudspeaker.

Bob shoved the atlas aside and hurried to the shelves where the encyclopedias were lined up. The article on Colombia in the *Americana* was pages long. The *Britannica* also devoted a fair amount of space to it. There wasn't enough time to read it all, and he couldn't take the reference books out of the library.

The overhead lights flicked again. Bob raced to the shelves where books on South America were kept and scooped off two volumes. One was titled *Colombia, Land of Contrasts*. The other was *Colombia, from New Granada to Bolivar.*

Bob snatched up his print-out and hurried to the check-out desk. A moment later he was taking his bike from the rack near the library entrance. He wished he had had time to browse through the books on Colombia. He probably hadn't chosen the most useful ones. Or perhaps he had. The books he had snatched up just might contain the clues that the Three Investigators needed to solve the mystery of the cranky collector.

Eager to begin reading, Bob pedaled off toward his home.

It was almost ten o'clock when Pete Crenshaw heard the footsteps. He and Marilyn Pilcher were in the living room of the Pilcher house. They had eaten fried chicken from the Cheerful Chicken carry-out place on the highway, and they had a fire going in the fireplace. The room was almost too warm, but the fire cast a nice glow and drove the shadows back to the corners.

Then the pacing began.

They were playing Trivial Pursuit and Marilyn was winning when the first steps came from above. Pete knew instantly that someone was moving about in the attic. In the silent house, the sound penetrated all the way to the first floor.

Pete's heart sank. He did not want to go upstairs. He disliked the Pilcher house. He disliked everything about it. It was cold and damp. It needed cleaning and airing out, and it had the sort of attic nobody needed—an attic where some unseen being had walked last night. True, Pete had not been on watch last night. He had not heard the restless pacing, but Bob and Jupe had told him about it.

And now it was starting again.

Marilyn looked up. "Did you hear it?" she said. She was whispering.

Pete wanted to say no, but he couldn't. He looked away from Marilyn and said nothing.

"Did you lock the back door?" Marilyn asked.

"I—I thought you did," he countered.

She stood up, looking toward the kitchen. "Someone could have come in."

"We'd have heard them," said Pete. "We'd have known it if the door opened."

But he went to the kitchen. The door was locked. The dead bolt was on. No one had come in.

Or had an intruder come in, then turned the dead bolt from the inside?

Marilyn came into the kitchen and stared

at the door. She frowned, then went back out. Pete followed her to the hall, where she stared up the stairs.

"Listen!" she said.

The footsteps were louder now. They made a hollow sound on the bare boards of the attic floor.

"Blast!" Marilyn went to the phone, lifted the receiver, and dialed 911. "I want to report a prowler," she said.

But was it a prowler? Pete wondered. Jupe said that last night no one came up the stairs and no one went down. Yet someone had walked in the attic, and walked and walked.

"Creepy!" said Pete out loud.

Marilyn ignored him. She was giving the address to the dispatcher on the other end of the line.

Pete started up the stairs. He was trembling and his throat was so dry that he couldn't swallow, but he went up anyway, step by step.

The pacing in the attic continued. A ghost? Or something more dangerous than a ghost?

Marilyn hung up the phone and followed Pete. She was no longer the arrogant rich girl. She was afraid, and she kept close to the big, athletic boy.

"When I was little," she said, "we had a

cook who got her jollies scaring kids. She told me this house was haunted."

"Did you have to bring that up now?" complained Pete.

The two stopped in the upper hall. The pacing stopped too. They listened.

Was there another listener above? Was someone waiting at the top of the attic stairs, leaning over the railing, ready to attack if anyone opened the attic door?

"I think we'll stay right here," Pete decided. He got a chair from the computer room, put it in the hall, and motioned for Marilyn to sit down.

"When the police get here," said Marilyn, "if there's nothing, like there's been nothing so far, you know what?"

"They'll think you're crazy," said Pete.

"Right. And sooner or later, they're going to stop coming. I'll call and they'll say it's just that nutty Pilcher kid and they won't answer the call."

"I think they have to answer calls," said Pete. "They can't take a chance you might be in danger. Only they'll look at you kind of funny when they show up."

He thought for a minute. What would Jupe do if he were here? He might look for some physical evidence he could show the officers—something they couldn't deny. Like a broken lock or . . . footprints! That was it! Footprints!

Pete remembered something he'd seen in Jeremy Pilcher's bathroom. When he was shut in there during the engagement party, he had noticed a can of talcum powder on the shelf over the basin.

Pete trotted through the collector's bedroom to the bathroom and snapped on the light. The powder was still there. He grabbed the can, carried it out to the hall, then sprinkled powder on the floor near the attic door.

Marilyn looked at him questioningly.

"If that's a real person up there, he can't get out without coming this way," said Pete. "If he's like other people, we'll see him—I hope. And he'll have to wade through the powder. He'll leave footprints and the cops will see the prints."

"Oh, right," said Marilyn. "Except, what do we say if he comes this way and there aren't any prints?"

Pete didn't answer. He heard a car pull into the drive. Car doors slammed. Someone began to circle the house, making sure no one was hiding in the shrubbery.

Marilyn Pilcher was halfway down the stairs when the doorbell rang. She opened the door to two uniformed men from the Rocky Beach Police Department. Pete heard her say, "Upstairs. In the attic. He's up there."

"All right," said one of the officers. He started up the stairs.

At that moment Pete heard the unknown intruder start down the attic stairs.

Pete turned to look at the door at the bottom of the stairs. In an instant it would open. The one who walked in the attic would be just a few feet away.

The officer on the main stairway must have heard the prowler coming. He drew his gun.

Pete heard a door open. However, the door did not move. There was only the sound of a knob turning.

The intruder stepped into the hall, still unseen. He walked past Pete and Pete felt cold—very cold. The one who paced so restlessly went down the stairs. He passed the officer who was looking desperately to the right and the left as if he would surely see who was making the footsteps if he only looked hard enough.

The officer shivered. He had felt the deadly chill, just as Pete had.

Pete looked at the floor where he had sprinkled the talcum. The powder was not disturbed. It lay like a light dusting of snow, with no mark to show that anything had come this way.

"Haunted!" croaked Pete. "This place really *is* haunted."

Downstairs in the hall, Marilyn Pilcher gave a whimper. "Stay here if you want to," she said. "I'm going home to my mother!"

10

JUPE ON DISPLAY

Jupe was three blocks behind when Ariago's car turned east on Santa Monica Boulevard. He was four blocks behind when Ariago slowed at Mayfield and drove into a parking building next to an enclosed shopping mall. An A. L. Becket store was at the west end of the complex. This could be the branch Ariago managed for Pilcher, thought Jupe. He locked his bike in a rack near the Becket store and went into the mall.

He was only minutes from Mrs. Pilcher's home. Why had Ariago gone there during business hours? Jupe wondered. And how often did he and Mrs. Pilcher meet? Ariago's past was unsavory. Why had he been visiting Jeremy Pilcher's ex-wife? Was she conspiring with him against Pilcher? If so, what did she hope to gain?

Jupe frowned. It would do no good to keep

going over the scant bits of information he had. He decided that he would try to see Ariago. He would explain that he and his friends wanted to help Marilyn Pilcher, and he would ask if Ariago knew anything about a bishop's book, or about Sogamoso or Navarro. Of course Ariago would be expecting these questions; no doubt Ariago had overheard Jupe's conversation with Mrs. Pilcher. Just the same, his reaction might be interesting. There was also a possibility that he might have some information that would lead Jupe to the truth.

The executive offices of the Becket store were on the third floor, behind the children's department. A woman smiled at Jupe from behind a desk and asked if she could help him. He handed her one of the cards of The Three Investigators and announced that he was Jupiter Jones, and that he needed to talk with Mr. Ariago.

The woman looked at the card and said, "Oh? Investigators?" Her tone was amused.

"It's about the disappearance of Jeremy Pilcher," said Jupiter. "I was at his daughter's engagement party yesterday. I met Mr. Ariago there."

"Mr. Pilcher?" Suddenly the woman stopped smiling. "He's disappeared?"

"Mr. Ariago knows the situation," said Jupiter.

When he did not say more she picked up a telephone, dialed an extension, then announced that Jupiter Jones was there to see Mr. Ariago. "It's about Mr. Pilcher," she said.

She listened for an instant, then put the phone down. "Mr. Ariago has a full schedule. He can't see you today."

"Oh?" In the past, many people had refused to see Jupe. He did not accept the rejections easily. Usually he found a way to get the interview he wanted; he planned to find a way today. Ariago might be ignorant of the secret files in Pilcher's computer. Perhaps he would be more reasonable if he knew about them.

"I know Mr. Ariago is a busy man," Jupe said, "but I think he'll see me when he learns I have information for him. It's from Mr. Pilcher's private files."

The woman smiled politely and said, "Why don't I just give him your message and your card and ask him to call you?"

Jupe saw that she was determined to guard her boss and keep Jupe away. He looked at his watch. After five. Office hours would be over soon. "I'll wait and catch him on the way out," said Jupe.

"You'll have quite a wait," the woman said with a laugh. "He stays till the store closes at nine."

Jupe left the executive offices and got on the down escalator, wondering what to do next. Should he give up and go home? Or wait for Ariago to appear at the close of business? Jupe weighed the choices as he rode past clothing and perfume on the second level and then down to furniture and appliances on level one.

Jupe finally decided to lie in wait for Ariago. By the time the store closed, the man should have seen Jupe's message about Pilcher's files. He might be nervous and willing to talk. If not, then the Investigators could maintain a surveillance on Ariago. There was something going on between him and Elizabeth Pilcher. It could have something to do with Jeremy Pilcher's kidnapping.

Jupe left Becket's and went into the mall. He had hours to kill. He looked at records and tapes and stereo equipment. He ate a couple of chili dogs. He tried on some sports clothes. He browsed through a bookstore and managed to skim half of a book he'd been meaning to read before the clerk started looking at him impatiently.

Jupe looked at his watch for the umpteenth time. Still more than an hour until Becket's closed. He went back into the department store and found a big leather-covered sofa in a secluded corner of the furniture department. He sat down to wait.

It was quiet in this corner of the store—very quiet. There were not many customers, and one lone salesman prowled the aisles. His feet made no noise on the carpeted floor. After a time Jupe's head drooped. He was tired. The prowler in the attic had kept him wide-eyed and edgy the night before, and now he was paying for it.

That attic—that was another mystery. What was happening in that attic? Did a ghost walk there?

Jupe reminded himself sternly that he did not believe in ghosts. People did not come back from the grave. The noise he'd heard must have been the old house creaking in protest as the night wind blew in off the ocean.

For a minute—just for a minute—Jupe felt himself doze off. For a minute he slept. Then he came awake with a start, and he opened his eyes.

It was dark. Jupe looked around and saw shapes—strange, black shapes. It took him a moment to recognize them. They were the shapes of bureaus and wing chairs and wardrobes.

Jupe went rigid with alarm. It was late! The store was closed, and he had slept right through the closing.

He stood up, listening. There must be a cleaning crew, but he did not hear them. There must be security people patrolling the store at night. Why hadn't they found him and roused him?

But they wouldn't have found him unless they took special care to see that no one was huddled on that particular sofa. It faced away from the aisle. Any watchman could walk within three feet of Jupe and not know he was there. The cleaning people could pass very close and never notice him.

Jupe rubbed his eyes. Beyond the bureaus and the wing chairs there was a light that shone with a dim red glow. A sign beneath the light said EXIT.

Jupe stumbled through the blackness toward the sign. When he reached the exit, he saw a second sign: EMERGENCY EXIT ONLY. ALARM WILL RING IF THIS DOOR IS OPENED.

Jupe imagined himself pushing open the door and stepping out into the mall. Bells would jangle. Lights would flash. No doubt there was a TV monitor where security men kept watch. The monitor would light up. The men would come running with their guns drawn. Before Jupe could find his way out of the building, he would be nabbed.

Jupe shuddered. A few months before, a Pasadena youth had been found in a mall after closing time. He had been charged with trespassing and attempted theft. The story had appeared in all the papers.

Jupe did not want to be featured in the local newspapers. How would it look for the head of an investigation firm to be apprehended at night in an empty department store?

Jupe turned away from the emergency exit and crept through the darkness to the main entrance of the store. But this was blocked by a huge steel shutter.

He went on, careful to make no noise, and found the employees' exit. This door also had the warning that an alarm would sound if it were opened.

A clock next to the employees' exit told him it was eleven P.M. Aunt Mathilda would be furious.

He searched until he found a pay phone. He put two dimes in the slot and dialed home. Aunt Mathilda answered. She sounded anxious and angry.

"Jupiter Jones, where are you?" she demanded.

"Marilyn Pilcher needed us," said Jupe. That was true enough so far as it went.

"Well, sometimes I need you, too," said Aunt Mathilda. "You never think of that. Are you at the Pilcher house with that poor girl? Is there any word of her father?"

"No, not yet. Listen, Aunt Mathilda, would you mind if I stayed over tonight? I really think I should."

"I do mind, but probably you should. All right, Jupiter. But be careful."

Aunt Mathilda hung up.

Jupe left the phone and felt his way back to the furniture department, back to the sofa. He was beginning to think of the sofa as his home base. He sat down, prepared to wait through the long hours until morning.

Soon he realized that he was hungry. He remembered reading a story about kids who were locked in a department store at night. They had raided the refrigerator in the store restaurant. But Jupe had not seen a restaurant when he went through the store that afternoon. He suspected that there was none. Becket's wouldn't need a restaurant; there were loads of food shops in the mall.

Should he go looking for food? There might be a candy counter or a department that sold gourmet foods.

He decided against it. It could be too risky.

His eyes closed. He dozed again, and he dreamed that he was at the Pilcher house and someone was knocking at the door. In his dream he knew who it was—it was Jeremy Pilcher. The old collector wanted to get in. "I'm coming!" cried Jupiter. "Don't go away! I'm coming!"

With a mighty effort he started upright. It was light! He saw people in front of him. They were staring at him, laughing, pointing. They were brisk morning people who wore business suits and carried newspapers. One of them was knocking and knocking at the window.

That window! There had been no window when he sat down yesterday evening. Why was there a window now?

He realized then that in the darkness he had gotten into a different part of the furniture department. He was not on the sofa he had chosen yesterday. He was on a different sofa. People were clustered outside to watch Jupe sleeping in Becket's display window!

Jupe jumped up. Any second the security people would come and grab him! The police would be summoned. They would send for Aunt Mathilda and Uncle Titus.

He heard the guards now. They were unlocking the employees' entrance.

Jupe ran and ducked behind a roll-top desk.

Someone hurried down the aisle. "He was

there!" said a man. "Right over there. He's here someplace!"

A second man passed close to the roll-top desk. "How come your crew didn't spot him last night?" a gruff voice demanded.

"We can't check every blasted chair in the place," said the first man.

When the men were past, Jupe put his head up and saw them near the display window. They were staring at the sofa as if it could tell them where he was.

Behind Jupe there was a new sound. Jupe looked around. A skinny man in an olive drab jump suit was at a control panel near the main entrance of the store. He was rolling up the great steel shutter that closed that entrance.

The way was clear.

Jupe leaped up and darted past the man in the jump suit. Someone yelled as he whizzed through the mall and out an automatic door to the parking area.

His bike was still there, locked to the rack. He almost dropped his keys in his eagerness, but he managed to get it unlocked. He yanked the bike free and pedaled away as a shout went up behind him.

Jupe did not look back. Sometimes it was wiser simply to run for your life!

11

THE BISHOP'S BOOK

"I do not believe in ghosts," announced Jupiter. He scowled at Pete.

"Okay, keep saying that," Pete shot back, "but if it wasn't a ghost, what was it? It walked past me in the hall, and I heard it but I couldn't see it. And I felt cold when it went by. I've heard those stories where the room gets cold when a ghost is there. I think the cop on the stairs felt it too. I saw him shiver."

"So he felt a draft," Bob put in. "You felt a draft. The Pilcher house is old and drafty."

The Three Investigators were in Headquarters. Jupe sat behind the desk looking rumpled and sleepy-eyed after his night in the department store. Pete was awake, but it was the wide-eyed, staring wakefulness of someone too keyed up to relax. Only Bob looked as if he had had a good night's rest.

Bob had brought his library books to Headquarters with him, and now he flipped one of them open.

"Do we really care if it was a ghost?" he said. "Any haunt who's hanging out in Pilcher's attic has probably been there for a long time. It didn't suddenly decide to snatch Mr. Pilcher off to the Twilight Zone. We're supposed to be finding the old man or finding the bishop's book. Maybe we can do that if we know more about the message on the computer. Now, guys, I don't want any cheering or clapping or anything, but I have found Sogamoso!"

Jupe was suddenly awake. "You know who Sogamoso is?"

"Not who," said Bob. "What. It's a small city in South America—in Colombia. Only forty-nine thousand people, give or take a few, so if Marilyn went there and asked about the old woman—well, some of the local citizens might know what she wanted."

"And she should watch out for Navarro while she's doing that," said Pete. "That's the warning in the computer letter."

"Okay, she asks for the old woman. She makes sure the person she asks isn't named Navarro," said Bob.

"No." Jupe shook his head. "Navarro isn't in Colombia. At least he wasn't in Colombia when Pilcher put that message into the computer. Pilcher wasn't sure Navarro was legal, and he mentioned the INS—and those initials almost always stand for the Immigration and Naturalization Service. So Navarro could be an undocumented alien, which means he was here in the United States."

"Okay," said Bob. "So until she leaves for Sogamoso, Marilyn watches out for an illegal immigrant named Navarro. Hey, maybe it was Navarro who tackled you in the attic, Jupe. Not the invisible guy who walked past Pete. The other one."

"He certainly wasn't a ghost, that one," said Jupe. "He was a real live person."

The telephone rang.

"Probably Marilyn wondering what we're doing," said Pete. "She went to her mom's house last night. Just wouldn't stay at her dad's any longer."

"I don't blame her," said Jupe.

But when he picked up the telephone, it was not Marilyn Pilcher calling. It was Luis Estava, the man the boys had known as Ray Sanchez.

Jupe had improvised a loudspeaker that allowed anyone in Headquarters to hear a telephone conversation. Now he put the receiver down on the loudspeaker so that Pete and Bob could listen.

"I'm surprised to hear from you, Mr. Estava," said Jupe. "Yesterday you walked out on us."

"Call me Ray, will you?" said Estava. "It's my middle name, and it's what my friends call me. And yesterday walking out seemed like the thing to do. Today I'm not sure. I just had a visit from the Rocky Beach Police Department. I didn't know they were that concerned about Pilcher's disappearance, but it looks like they're moving on it. It also looks like I'm a suspect."

"You had a motive for harming Pilcher," Jupe pointed out.

"Well, yes," admitted Estava. "I did want the old creep to pay for wrecking my dad's business, but to pay the same way—business-wise. I'd have to be sicker than he is to hurt him physically. He's an old man!"

There was sincere indignation in his tone. Jupe glanced at his friends.

"Sounds like he means it," Bob murmured.

Jupe nodded. "All right, we believe you. But why are you calling? You can't really care what we think."

"I do care," said Estava. "Marilyn seems to have faith in you, and I guess I do too. I want to say that if I can help find Old Man Pilcher, I will. Unless somebody locates the old pirate, I may spend the rest of my life being a suspect. So if you think of anything I can do, just call."

"I can think of something right now," said Jupiter. "Do you know anything about Soga-moso?"

"Soga—soga who?" said Estava.

Jupe repeated the name. It meant nothing to Estava. Neither did Navarro. "I know a few people named Navarro," admitted the secretary. "In some areas it's like being named Jones. None of my friends know Pilcher, however."

"Did you ever hear Mr. Pilcher mention tears of the gods?" asked Jupe.

"Tears of the gods? You're kidding."

"No. The tears, whatever they are, seemed very important to Mr. Pilcher."

"I'm sorry," said Estava. "I can't recall a thing."

"One more question," said Jupe. "Soga-moso is in Colombia, and Colombia is a major source of cocaine. Is there any chance that Mr. Pilcher was involved in drug traffic?"

"Absolutely not. He was violently opposed to drugs," said Estava. "Pilcher used to fire employees just because they were rumored to use illegal drugs. Check with Marilyn if you don't want to take my word for it."

Jupe thanked him. Estava then gave Jupiter his telephone number and hung up.

"This case is full of loose ends," said Jupe, "and none of them seem to connect anywhere. I don't think we're any closer to finding Mr. Pilcher than we were two days ago."

"I bet Sogamoso isn't going to help us either," said Pete. "By the time Marilyn goes there and finds the right old woman, her dad could be dead."

"Of natural causes," agreed Bob, "like old age. Okay, what's the next step?"

"Mrs. Pilcher suggested that we search the *Bonnie Betsy*," said Jupiter. "We have already been over the house with a fine-tooth comb, so why not try the yacht? Marilyn must know where it's moored."

"And if we find the bishop's book, she may get her dad back," said Bob. "Then he can tell her firsthand about the old woman and the tears of the gods."

Jupiter called Mrs. Pilcher's house in Santa Monica. Marilyn answered the telephone. She told them her father's yacht was in dry dock at the Central Coast Marine Corporation. "It's that shipyard on Bowsprit Drive," she said. "I'll phone there and tell them you're coming so they'll let you go aboard the yacht."

Soon the boys were riding their bikes up the Coast Highway. Twenty minutes of brisk pedaling brought them to the Bowsprit Drive turnoff.

Bowsprit ran onto a man-made finger of land that jutted out from the shore for more than a mile. A yacht club and a series of ships' chandlers occupied the south side of this jetty. On the north were several ship-yards. Central Coast Marine was about a quarter mile in from the highway. It was protected by a businesslike cyclone fence and by a gate where a uniformed security man kept watch from a small guardhouse.

Jupiter and his friends skidded to a halt at the gate and Jupe identified himself to the guard.

"Oh, yes, Miss Pilcher phoned," said the man. "I was expecting somebody older, but if Miss Pilcher says it's okay to let you in, I guess it's okay. Sign in here."

He thrust a notebook at them. They signed the book and he noted the time beside their signatures, then took a bunch of keys from a pegboard behind him and held them out to Jupe. "The cabins and the wheelhouse on the *Bonnie Betsy* are locked. You'll need these."

He pointed to the right. "Go down that

way past that schooner—you see the one that's having her bottom scraped?—and you'll see the *Bonnie Betsy*. She's in the dry dock down the quay. You can't miss her. Big ship with a black hull and the name in gold on her stern."

The boys thanked him and rode on, feeling the breeze that came fresh from the ocean. Gulls circled and swooped overhead, screaming harshly. The air was now filled with the smell of kelp and the fishy odor of the barnacles drying on the hulls of the boats that had been hauled out of the water for repairs.

Most of the boats the boys passed were large sailboats, wooden or fiberglass pleasure craft from forty to sixty feet long. The *Bonnie Betsy*, when they found her, turned out to be quite different. She was practically a small ocean liner. She had a black steel hull and a white-painted superstructure that gave her the look of a luxury cruise ship.

"Wow!" said Pete. "Old Man Pilcher wasn't kidding around when he bought that one!"

"He didn't pinch pennies there," said Bob.

The ship had not been hoisted out of the water like the smaller yachts the boys had seen. Instead she had been floated into a huge concrete trench called a dry dock. Gigantic waterproof gates on the seaward side of the trench had been closed. The water had been pumped out, leaving the *Bonnie Betsy* high and dry. She rested now on steel struts inside the dry dock.

A gangway led from the quay to the ship. Jupe was the first to cross. As he stepped onto the deck of Pilcher's vessel he let out a small sound that was part surprise and part disappointment.

"What's the matter?" asked Bob.

"Nothing, I guess. I just expected it to feel the way boats usually feel when you step aboard. You know how they seem to be alive? Everything moves just a little. This is so . . . so dead!"

"Yeah," Pete agreed. "Like they built it on solid ground with a basement that goes down thirty feet."

The boys went forward and up a ladder to the bridge, and Jupe tried the keys that the security man had given him. When he found the right one, he opened the door to the wheelhouse. They went in and saw plate-glass windows that were streaked and salty. There were cabinets with drawers under the windows. The wheelhouse itself was trim and shipshape.

"I was expecting more of a mess," said Bob. "Mr. Pilcher has so much stuff every-where."

"Maybe he feels differently about ships," said Jupe. "Ships aren't supposed to be hip-deep in clutter."

"Or maybe he hired someone to be skipper and the guy wouldn't let him mess up the bridge," Pete suggested.

Jupe opened a drawer in one of the cabinets. He saw maps neatly lined up, one on top of the other. Jupe thumbed through them. They were nautical charts showing reefs and shallows. Several were for the waters off the coast of South America.

"I wonder how often he went to Colombia," Jupe said.

"Sogamoso isn't a port city," Bob told him. "If he wanted to get there, he'd have to travel in from the coast—or maybe from one of the ports in Venezuela."

"Hey, I thought we were here to find a bishop's book," said Pete. "Where is it?"

"Good question." Bob began to open one drawer after another, to shuffle through charts. Pete peered into storage cabinets. Jupe checked some open shelves. The boys found books on navigation and some navigational instruments but nothing that could possibly connect to a bishop.

When they had searched every inch of the wheelhouse, Jupe locked the door and the boys climbed down the ladder to the main deck. Cabins opened onto the decks on both sides of the ship. The boys started going through them.

Most appeared to have been unused. Bunks and beds were stripped. Mattresses were turned up. There were signs that the crew's quarters had been occupied fairly recently. One of the crewmen had left a rumpled T-shirt under his bunk. Crumpled cigarette packs and bits of paper still sat in the wastebaskets.

The Investigators came at last to a cabin that was larger than the others. Blinds were pulled down over windows and the place was quite dark. When Jupe flipped a switch beside the door, there was no flood of light.

"I guess there's no power aboard the *Bonnie Betsy* right now," said Jupe. "She really is a dead ship."

Leaving the door open so that there would be more light, he went into the cabin. A wide bed was covered with a sheet of plastic. Plastic sheets shrouded chairs and draped tables as well. On the far side of the cabin were shelves and shelves, each with a small ledge in front to keep objects from falling off when the seas were rough.

Jupe saw a flashlight on one of the shelves. He picked it up and snapped it on, then swept the beam back and forth.

"Yep, this is Old Man Pilcher's cabin!" said Pete.

The shelves were jammed with the clutter that the boys now associated with the old collector. Books and papers were stuck in every which way. A couple of battered tennis balls were crammed in among the books. One leather glove nestled close to a bowling trophy that the Westside Keglers' Club had awarded to Ernest J. Krebs.

"Why would Pilcher keep a bowling trophy someone else won?" Bob wondered.

"Because it was there," said Pete.

Jupe stepped forward toward the trophy and almost stumbled over a pile of things on the floor. One of the shelves had split and pulled away from the bulkhead behind it. It had sagged outward, spilling books and papers onto the carpeting. Jupe bent to pick up a book from the top of the pile. It was an extremely old book with a leather cover that was fastened shut with a clasp. The clasp gave out a dull golden gleam when Jupe shone the flashlight on it. The cover was so old that it left flakes of rusty leather on Jupe's fingers.

Jupe frowned at the design embossed in the leather on the front of the book. It was shaped like a tall, pointed cap. There was a cross on the front of the cap.

Jupe looked toward his friends. "I think this is a picture of a miter," he said. "That's the sort of cap a bishop wears. I think we've found the bishop's book!"

He turned toward the door, ready to go out on deck. But his way was blocked. A man stood in the doorway, a husky man with broad shoulders that stretched the cloth of a blue work shirt.

"What've you got there?" said the man. He held out a huge calloused hand. "You aren't going anyplace with that. Give it here!"

12
TEARS OF THE GODS

Jupe tried to hold on to the book. He couldn't. The man in the blue shirt yanked him out onto the deck, then wrestled the book away. There wasn't a thing Jupe could do about it. Two more husky men had appeared. One of them had a length of pipe. He held it loosely in one hand and slapped it into his other palm. He looked longingly at Jupe, as if he really wanted to bring the pipe down on Jupe's head.

"We're fed up with you kids coming over the fence and wrecking stuff," he said. "This time we're not just going to toss you out the gate. This time you're going to stay for a while and find out what happens to vandals."

"We are not vandals!" Jupe was indignant. "We are here at the request of Miss Marilyn Pilcher. We signed in properly. Ask the man at the gate."

The men looked at one another doubtfully, none willing to admit he might be making a mistake.

"If any harm comes to us, you'll have to answer to Miss Pilcher," said Jupe.

"And that's just for openers," Pete declared.

"We're friends of Police Chief Reynolds," added Bob. "Go ahead! Call the Rocky Beach Police Department and tell them you've got Jupiter Jones and Pete Crenshaw and Bob Andrews. See what they say!"

"What do you think, Bo?" said one of the men.

"They're snowin' us," said the man who had the book. Just the same, he looked back toward the gate where the boys had checked in.

"I'm goin' to make sure," said the third man. He set out at a trot for the gate.

The others waited, and in minutes the big man was back. The gateman was with him. He looked at the boys, gave a quick nod, and said, "Yeah, that's them. I let 'em through myself not half an hour ago."

"Oh." The fellow with the book seemed very disappointed. "Okay, you can go back to whatever you were doing," he said.

"I'd like that book, if you don't mind," said Jupiter.

The man handed it over. "Sorry, kid, but we've had a lot of trouble here."

The men drifted off and the security guard returned to his post. Jupe and his friends watched them go. When they had disappeared into the jungle of beached yachts that covered the quay, Jupe took a deep breath and looked at the book in his hands.

"You're shaking," Pete accused.

"Nonsense!" said Jupiter, mentally telling his hands to hold steady. "Those men were bluffing. They wouldn't have done anything."

He pried open the catch that held the book closed and lifted the front cover. The spine creaked as if it might split and send pages raining down onto the deck. But the book didn't come apart, and Jupe began to turn the pages. They felt as fragile as autumn leaves, dry, ready to crumble. A gap in the middle of the book showed where some pages had been cut out.

"It's a diary, or something like a diary," said Jupe. "It's handwritten, and there are dates. It starts with '*Enero*.' That's Spanish for January. On January first the bishop—if he's the one who wrote the book—he was at . . . at a place called Santa Fe de Bogotá."

"Bingo!" cried Bob. "Bogotá's in Colombia. So there's the link with Sogamoso. Sogamoso is in Colombia too."

"Right!" Jupe was trying to appear calm, but his eyes sparkled. "So we may assume that the computer message has something to do with Jeremy Pilcher's kidnapping. In fact, it may have *everything* to do with it."

"But what about that book?" said Pete. "Jupe, you can read Spanish. What's it all about?"

Jupe frowned. A lot of the words were unfamiliar. And the ink was faded and brown. The writing was crabbed and the pages were crowded with the old script—so crowded that lines ran together. "I don't think I can read this," Jupe confessed. "I'm not sure I could read it even if it were in English."

Bob looked over his shoulder. "Yeah!" he said. "It looks like one of those old documents where they made all the *s*'s look like *f*'s."

"So what are we waiting for?" Pete demanded. "I'll bet if we ask Dr. Barrister, he'll know somebody who reads that stuff."

He was speaking of Dr. Henry Barrister, a professor of anthropology at Ruxton University in the nearby San Fernando Valley. Dr. Barrister had helped the boys in the past when they needed information on folk medicine and magic and witchcraft. He had many friends on the Ruxton faculty, and their specialized knowledge was a boon to the young investigators.

"Dr. Barrister might save us a lot of time," Jupe conceded. "We can't take the book to Ruxton, however, before we talk to Marilyn Pilcher. She asked us to find the bishop's book so that she could use it to ransom her father. Perhaps she doesn't care why the kidnapper wants the book, just so long as her father is safe."

"Oh, yeah," said Pete. "Sometimes I forget about the kidnapping. I mean, it doesn't seem like anybody really likes old Pilcher. It's easy to get carried away solving the puzzle and forget why we're on the case!"

Jupe nodded, and locked the door of Pilcher's cabin. Then the boys turned in the keys at the gate and located a pay phone. First they tried to call Marilyn Pilcher at her mother's house in Santa Monica again, but this time they only reached the answering machine. Jupe left a message, then called the Pilcher house in Rocky Beach.

Mrs. McCarthy picked up that phone. "Wait a minute and I'll get her for you."

When Marilyn came on the line, Jupe told her about finding what appeared to be the journal of a bishop. Marilyn said nothing for a moment, but Jupe heard her draw in a deep breath. She was like a swimmer who had been too long underwater; now she had come to the surface and could breathe again.

"Thank goodness!" she said at last.

"We wondered," said Jupe. "Do you want to find out why the book is so important, or do you want to turn it over to the kidnapper and just not worry about it?"

Marilyn hesitated. "We have a little time," she said. "That man called again. I told him we were still trying to find the book, only it was hard when we don't know exactly what we're looking for, and he said, 'One more day. You have one more day. I will not wait longer.' "

"So we have until tomorrow," said Jupe. He then explained about Dr. Barrister. "He must know people who can read old manuscripts. Shall we take the book to Ruxton?"

"Maybe you'd better," said Marilyn after a pause. "If we give away something that my dad really wants, he would have a fit. Even if we save his life, he could have a fit. He's like that. So go ahead. We've got nothing to lose because I have no way to contact this guy, whoever he is, to let him know we've got the thing."

She stopped for a second, then went on, "I probably shouldn't have the book here in the house anyway. Somebody was here while I was with my mom last night. Somebody searched my room. I could see that my bureau drawers were different, like somebody took stuff out and then put it back. If it was the man who has Dad, he's also got Dad's keys, doesn't he? He can come and go as he pleases."

"Call a locksmith," said Jupe. "Have the locks changed. Okay, we'll try Dr. Barrister and we'll let you know."

Next, Jupe phoned Dr. Barrister at Ruxton. He was in luck. Even though summer vacation had started, the professor was still coming into his office every day. He promised to wait for the boys.

The Investigators hurried back to the salvage yard and begged Uncle Titus for a ride.

"You need a lift out to Ruxton?" said Uncle Titus. He grinned and pulled at the end of his big mustache. "I promised your Aunt Mathilda I'd deliver some bricks to a man in North Hollywood," he said. "I'll have to pass right by Ruxton. The truck is loaded already. Come on. Don't dillydally. Let's go!"

The three boys scrambled into the back of the smaller salvage-yard truck, and they were off down the highway. In less than an hour Uncle Titus deposited them on the Ruxton campus, promising to return a little later.

Dr. Barrister was in his office with a friend—a skinny man with a very bald, very shiny head. "This is Dr. Edouard Gonzaga," said Dr. Barrister. "Dr. Gonzaga heads up our Department of Romance Languages. He has a special interest in old Spanish manuscripts."

Jupe beamed. He produced the bishop's book and handed it to Dr. Gonzaga.

Dr. Gonzaga opened the book and looked at the first page. "Ah!" he said. He turned the page, and then another and another. A huge smile lit up his whole face. "Incredible!" he exclaimed.

"What is it?" asked Jupe.

"January first, at Santa Fe de Bogotá," said Dr. Gonzaga, turning back to the first page. "The author writes of saying Mass and of praying for the people of New Granada that God might bless their efforts. After Mass there was waiting at the palace a letter from His Most Gracious Majesty King Carlos."

Dr. Gonzaga looked up from the book. "You may have a real treasure here," he said. "The author of this journal probably *was* a bishop. He writes about a palace, and a bishop's residence is always called a palace. His Majesty wrote to him, which is hardly a thing that would happen if he were only a humble priest. It will have to be verified, of course; there are ways to find out how old a book is. We can analyze the paper and the inks and so forth. But it seems you may have the missing diary of Enrique Jiminez, the bloodstained bishop!"

"The bloodstained bishop?" echoed Jupe.

Pete gulped. "Wh-why was he bloodstained?" he asked. "Did something happen to him?"

"Eventually, my boy, something happens to all of us," said Dr. Gonzaga. "Life is a terminal affair, and no one gets out of it alive. The bloodstained bishop caught a cold. In the old days a cold could be serious indeed. It could easily become pneumonia, and that was often fatal. There were rumors that one of the unfortunate prelate's servants neglected him as he lay sick, and so hastened his death. No one was certain. The only thing that was known at the time was that the bishop's manservant disappeared after the bishop's death. Several members of his household told how Bishop Jiminez wrote every day in his journal, but no journal was ever found."

Dr. Barrister beamed at the Three Investigators. "There's a mystery for you," he said. "You boys should love it! Of course, it's about four hundred years old, and by this time the clues are very cold."

"Gold might be involved," said Dr. Gonzaga. "When the Spaniards marched through South America, claiming lands left and right for their king and queen, gold was often involved. Shiploads of it left the New World bound for Spain. The Spaniards took what they could find, then pressed the Indians into service and forced them to mine more. This Bishop Jiminez was said to be cruel to the Indians who worked in the gold mines. That was the reason they called him the bloodstained bishop. Whether he was really to blame, or whether it was the agents of the Spanish king—the overseers who supervised the work at the mines—well, after hundreds of years, who can be sure?

"At any rate, the bishop was supposed to have regretted the harshness. In his old age he worked to improve the conditions of the Indians. Unfortunately people often pay more attention to wickedness than to repentance. It is the bloodstained bishop that people remember today, and not the kindly reformer."

The boys were silent for a moment, thinking of the long-ago events and wondering how they might have supplied the motive for the recent crime of kidnapping.

"If that book really is the missing diary of Bishop Jiminez, would it be very valuable?" Jupe asked at last.

Dr. Gonzaga looked doubtful. "Valuable? Well, that's one of those relative terms. It would be of interest to scholars and historians, but it wouldn't be a fabulous find—not like a draft of the Magna Charta or a letter from Queen Isabella to Christopher Columbus, for example. Nobody would pay a fortune for it."

Dr. Gonzaga tucked the book under his arm. "But to a scholar?" he said. "Fascinating! I can't wait to sit down with this and start working on a translation and—"

"Oh, no!" cried Bob.

"There isn't time!" said Pete.

"I beg your pardon?" Dr. Gonzaga's smile disappeared.

"The most recent owner of the book has been kidnapped," said Jupe. "The kidnapper is demanding the bishop's book as ransom. If the book isn't turned over to the kidnapper tomorrow, there is no telling what might happen."

"Oh," said Dr. Gonzaga. "I see. I . . . don't suppose there's time to make a photocopy? No, of course not. This sort of book has to be sent to a lab to be photographed properly. A Xerox machine wouldn't do."

Dr. Gonzaga took the book from under his arm. For a few moments he stared at it as if it were a priceless treasure. Then, with a sigh, he handed it to Jupe.

"I hope it won't vanish again," he said. "If by any chance you can save it . . ."

"Of course," said Jupiter. "You'll be one of the first to know."

The boys started for the door. But Jupe turned back suddenly. "Do you know anything about tears of the gods?" he asked.

"Tears of the gods?" echoed Dr. Gonzaga. "That's a name that some Indians in Colombia give to emeralds. Why do you ask? Does it have anything to do with the book?"

"It might!" said Jupiter.

13

SETTING A TRAP

"Emeralds!" Bob leaned back in his chair and grinned at the ceiling in Headquarters. "Spanish conquerors! A stolen diary! A vanishing servant! What a case this is! Wait till Mr. Sebastian hears about it."

Hector Sebastian was a mystery writer and a friend of the boys. He always took a lively interest in their cases.

Jupe chuckled. "Mr. Sebastian would probably like us to wait," he said, "at least until we put all the pieces of the puzzle together."

He had the print-out of the computer message on the desk in front of him. "Tears of the gods," he said. "And all for Marilyn, according to this message. But where are the tears? And what does the bloodstained bishop have to do with them?"

"There are lots of emeralds in Colombia," said Bob. "According to those library books I read, Colombia is the biggest producer of emeralds in the world. Sounds like Marilyn has to go to Sogamoso to find them. I wonder if that bishop had anything to do with emerald mining, or was it just gold?"

"If Pilcher is giving Marilyn a bunch of emeralds," said Pete, "she could be one really rich lady."

Jupe looked at his watch. "It's getting late. The afternoon is practically gone. We'd better call her and tell her what we know so far," he said. He pulled the telephone toward him and dialed the number of the Pilcher house. Marilyn answered on the second ring.

"It's me," said Jupe. "You sound jumpy. Did you hear from the kidnapper again?"

"No, but I'm not leaving the phone. Did you find out anything from your friend at Ruxton?"

"We did. The book we found may be the diary of a bishop who lived in Colombia a few hundred years ago. He was called the bloodstained bishop because he was cruel to the Indians who worked the gold mines there. The diary disappeared when the bishop died. We can't be absolutely sure about any of this without leaving the book with Dr. Barrister's friend Dr. Gonzaga so he can have it analyzed. We didn't want to do that."

"You bet you didn't," said Marilyn.

"One more thing," said Jupiter. "We know about the tears of the gods. It's the way the Indians in the Andes refer to emeralds."

"Emeralds, huh?" Marilyn was silent for a second, then she said, "Well! Emeralds. I wonder what Dad meant. Is he leaving me a bunch of emeralds? And what's all the mumbo jumbo about an old woman and midsummer's day? It sounds like witch-craft—you know, like I'm supposed to go to the crossroads by the light of the moon and bury a rabbit's foot—that kind of stuff."

"After we ransom your father, it may all become clear," said Jupe. "Right now the important thing is that we have the book, so we *can* pay the ransom. Are you going to spend the night at your father's house? Do you want someone to stay with you?"

"My mom said she'd come over, so I'll be okay," Marilyn said. "I'll let you know as soon as I hear anything."

She hung up.

Almost immediately the phone rang. It was Harry Burnside calling. "Marilyn Pil-cher paid me the balance due on her party," he said. "I am solvent, at least for now, and

I'm balancing my books. Want to drop by the shop so I can give you guys the money I owe you?"

"Sure thing," said Jupe.

He hung up, then locked the diary in the file cabinet. The boys went out through Tunnel Two to the workshop, where they got their bikes.

Burnside's catering place was on a side street in Rocky Beach. When the boys arrived, there was no one in the front of the shop, so they went through to the kitchen. They found Harry Burnside there, sitting at a butcher block table with his pen in hand and an account book open in front of him. One of the girls who had waited on the guests at Marilyn Pilcher's party was just leaving. She waved a quick greeting.

Burnside smiled. "Hi," he said. "I've got your money ready, and you'd better get it while it's going. I figure I owe you for four and a half hours at minimum wage, plus a bit." He handed an envelope to each of them.

"That takes care of everyone but Ramon, and I'll pay him as soon as he gets back from making a delivery."

"Ramon?" said Jupe. "Oh! Ramon's the dishwasher you hired, isn't he?"

"Yup. He's been helping me out the last couple of weeks, off and on."

Bob opened his envelope and thumbed through the bills there. "Hey, you gave me too much," he said.

"Minimum wage plus a bit," Harry Burnside shot back. "I can't stand to pay just minimum wage. It makes me feel like I'm running the Ebenezer Scrooge Sweatshop. You want some chocolate cake? It's left over from a kid's party I did this afternoon, and I don't dare eat it. My girl will dump me if I gain one more ounce."

"Funny, Aunt Mathilda said something like that to me this morning at breakfast," said Jupe, "but I don't think she really meant it."

"The cake's in the pantry," said Burnside. "On the shelf behind the door."

Jupe went into the pantry, a square little room that opened off the kitchen. It had floor-to-ceiling shelves where Burnside kept packages of chocolate and canisters of flour and sugar, tins of caviar and jars of olives.

Jupe had to swing the door half shut to get at the chocolate cake. As he reached for the knife that Burnside had left on the cake plate, his foot touched something soft.

He looked down and saw a plastic sack that had been shoved behind the door. It was a pink sack with brilliant purple lettering on it. A sack from Becket's Department Store.

For a second Jupe just stared at the bag. So
Harry Burnside has been at Becket's, he
thought. Well, why not? Why shouldn't the
caterer go into the department store to pick
up something he needed—a new shirt perhaps, or a pair of shoes. What if Ariago did
manage a Becket store for Jeremy Pilcher?
That didn't mean Burnside and Ariago had
business together.

But in his mind's eye Jupe saw Ariago
hurrying away from Mrs. Pilcher's house. He
kept coming back to that memory. Where
had Ariago been while Jupe and Mrs. Pilcher
talked? Had he been hiding somewhere, listening?

Hiding! There was no other word for it. If
Ariago had just been a casual visitor, he
would have been in the living room. Jupe
would have seen him. But he had hidden.
Why?

And could Harry Burnside be involved
with him? Could the good-natured caterer
have had a part in Pilcher's abduction? It
was an outside chance. True, Burnside's
name was not on the list in Pilcher's computer, but that meant only that Pilcher didn't
know Burnside well enough to have him
investigated. It did not mean Burnside
wasn't interested in Pilcher. He might have a
relative whom Pilcher had wronged. Or he

might know something about the blood-stained bishop and the mysterious diary. Or Ariago might have bribed him. Burnside needed money; he might have been willing to take a bribe.

There was something blue at the top of the plastic sack. Jupe bent and touched it. It was a Windbreaker. The sack fell sideways and the Windbreaker tumbled out. Under the Windbreaker was a folded newspaper. Jupe did not touch this; he just stared at it.

Bits had been cut from the paper. Words! Someone had cut words from the headlines on the front page!

MAYOR OF TOKYO   TO HUNTINGTON HARBOR
BRINGS GREETINGS TO SISTER CITY

That was one headline, and mentally Jupe supplied the word that had been cut out. It was "comes." It was the second word in the note from the kidnapper.

"Hey, Jupe!" Burnside called from the kitchen. "You going to take all day cutting that cake?"

Jupe jumped. He stuffed the Windbreaker back into the sack and propped the sack against the wall. Hastily he hacked three slices from the cake, put the slices on a paper plate, and carried the plate to the kitchen.

"I didn't cut any for you," he told Burnside.

"Thanks," said Burnside. "My good resolutions don't last long without lots of reinforcement."

Bob and Pete took their cake. Jupe pulled a stool from under a counter and sat down to eat his.

"So how are you guys doing with the heiress?" asked Burnside. "You got any leads yet? Is she going to get her father back?"

"She's going to try, but it's an uphill job," said Jupe. "The kidnapper wants a thing called the bishop's book as ransom, and Marilyn doesn't know what that means."

Bob and Pete stopped eating for a second. Pete drew a breath as if to say, "But we do know!"

He didn't say it. Instead he said, "I'll bet we've looked at about seven billion books."

"And a few tons of old papers," Bob put in. "Mr. Pilcher sure glommed onto stuff and never let go."

Burnside chuckled. "I'll bet most of it isn't worth a darn," he said.

"Later on we're going to Central Coast Marine," said Jupe. "You know, that shipyard up on Bowsprit Drive? Pilcher has a yacht in dry dock there. The *Bonnie Betsy*. Mrs. Pilcher suggested that we search there for the book. I guess the yacht's as full of junk as the house."

"Be surprised if it wasn't," said Burnside. He looked past Jupe to the doorway. "Ramon, come on in," he said. "I've got your money ready for you."

Jupe turned to see the dark-haired fellow who had washed dishes at the Pilcher party. He nodded to the boys and went to take an envelope from Burnside.

"You guys almost ready?" Jupe asked his friends. He ate the last of his cake, and Pete and Bob hastily finished theirs. They said good-bye to Harry Burnside and Ramon, who was in the pantry cutting some cake for himself.

The Three Investigators went out the back way. They passed Burnside's truck, which was parked in the alley, and kept going until they were out of the alley and across the street. Only then did Jupe look back.

"Now what was all that double-talk?" Bob demanded.

"Yeah? Why'd you give Burnside that business about the bishop's book, and how we're going to the shipyard later?" said Pete. "You know something we don't?"

"There was a plastic sack in the pantry," said Jupe. "It was from Becket's. Ariago manages Becket's. That might not mean a thing, except that there's a newspaper in the sack with words cut out of some of the headlines."

Bob gasped. "The ransom note!"

"Exactly," Jupe said.

"Burnside?" said Pete. "Burnside a kidnapper? I can't believe that. It's like believing your grandpa is really Dracula!"

"I know." Jupe looked grim. "It doesn't seem possible, but I saw the paper. I have to believe what I saw."

"So you're setting a trap for him," Bob prompted.

"Right. He thinks the book may be at the shipyard. Now let's see what he does."

Pete looked worried. "If we're going to follow him, we need a car—right away!"

Jupe nodded. "Ray Estava said he wants to help us. Let's give him a chance!"

14
JUPE THINKS AGAIN

Ray Estava was there in fifteen minutes. He drove a dull-looking gray sedan that had rust on the fenders and a few dents and nicks on the side panels. "I borrowed it from a neighbor," said Estava as the boys got in. "It's such a nothing sort of car, no one will ever notice us. Who are we going to tail?"

"Harry Burnside," Jupe told him. "His shop's over there. He should be leaving any minute."

"Burnside?" Sanchez looked startled. "He's mixed up in this mess? But he's the original Mr. Nice Guy!"

"I know it's hard to believe," Jupe admitted, "but I found the evidence. . . . Look! There he is!"

Jupe pointed. They could see the back door of the catering shop. Harry Burnside was just locking the dead bolt.

146

Ray Estava started his car.

Burnside got into his truck, and the truck rolled forward.

The boys ducked down out of sight.

Burnside braked at the end of the alley and looked to the left and the right. Then he pulled out and headed for the Coast Highway.

Estava let him get a block ahead before he followed.

Burnside had to wait for a light at the highway intersection. Estava slowed so that a van loaded with surfers could pass and get between his car and Burnside's truck.

"You're pretty good at this," said Pete admiringly.

"I see lots of spy movies," said Estava.

The light changed. They moved out onto the highway, heading north toward Bowsprit. Jupe tensed as they neared the turnoff. But the catering truck sailed right past Bowsprit and sped on up the highway.

"Hey!" said Bob. "That wasn't in the script!"

Jupe didn't answer.

At Chaparral Canyon, Burnside braked and turned right. Three blocks from the highway there was a condo complex. Burnside parked in front and went up to the entrance, where he rang a bell.

Estava drove past Burnside's truck. He parked on the next block, and the boys watched through the rear window. They saw Burnside go into the condo complex. After a few minutes he came out again with a girl— a pretty girl with long dark hair. The two got into the catering truck, and it made a U-turn and headed back toward the highway.

"He's not going to the shipyard," Bob predicted. "Not tonight."

Burnside didn't. He drove south to Marina del Rey, where he and the girl went up to a restaurant.

"So much for that," said Ray Estava. "He's just taking his girl out for dinner. I'm not surprised—he's no crook. If he'd gone to that shipyard, I think I'd have had a heart attack!"

As Estava spoke Burnside paused in the restaurant doorway for a second, holding the door open so that his girl could go ahead of him. He had his head turned away from the watchers in Estava's car, and for an instant Jupe recalled Jeremy Pilcher standing in his kitchen doorway with his head turned toward Burnside and the dishwasher, Ramon. For an instant Jupe again saw Ramon's face as the man looked at Pilcher. Estava's words "heart attack" echoed in Jupe's mind.

"Oh!" Jupe struck his forehead with his

fist. "How dumb could I be? Of course it wasn't Burnside! It couldn't be him. I remember now. Pilcher went to the kitchen to raise Cain because one of the waitresses broke a glass—that's the moment it all began!"

He was silent for a moment. He concentrated, his eyes closed. "Harry Burnside was there," he said. "He was putting food on the trays, and the guy called Ramon was at the sink with his hands all wet and soapy. Until that second there was no kidnapping plot. I'd bet my life on it. Pilcher wasn't in any danger—and then suddenly he was in deadly danger, and he knew it. I saw it happen, but I didn't understand."

Bob sat forward. "What didn't you understand?" he asked. "What happened?"

"Remember how angry Pilcher was? He was shouting, and Marilyn was trying to calm him down. Then Ramon looked at him and Ramon dropped a plate. Pilcher almost had a heart attack on the spot."

"Nothing odd about that," said Ray Estava. "It almost killed the old geezer when things got broken—especially if there was a chance he'd have to pay for the breakage."

"That wasn't it!" Jupe insisted. "The instant the dish smashed, Pilcher really noticed Ramon for the first time. Ramon was staring at him. I couldn't see Pilcher's face, but I saw Ramon, and he had a strange expression on his face. I thought at the time that he was afraid, but I was wrong. It wasn't fear I saw—it was hatred. He was looking at Pilcher the way you'd look at a worm that needed to be stepped on! Ramon recognized Pilcher. He knew him. And Pilcher recognized Ramon. That's why he had the angina attack!"

Bob gasped. "Then Ramon is—he's Navarro!" he said.

"He could be," said Jupe. "He could be the one Marilyn Pilcher was warned about. And unless I am very mistaken, he's now at Central Coast Marine searching the *Bonnie Betsy*. He came back to Burnside's in time to hear me talk about the yacht."

"Let's go!" Estava shifted to drive and stepped on the gas, and they roared back toward Bowsprit.

It was almost dark when they approached Central Coast Marine. Pete worried that the security man would never let them through the gate.

"We won't need to go through the gate," said Jupe. "Look!"

The others saw it. Burnside's disreputable dishwasher was caught in the glare of Estava's headlights. He was straddling the

chain link fence that surrounded the shipyard.

"Don't stop now!" cried Bob. "Don't let
him know we noticed. Unless maybe we
want to tackle him and make him tell us
where Pilcher is?"

"Better to follow him," said Jupe.

Estava drove past Ramon. The boys looked
out the back window and saw the man drop
from the top of the fence to the ground
outside the yard. He took off at a run toward
the highway.

Estava went into a tight U-turn. He cut his
bright lights and was using only his parking
lights when they passed Ramon again. The
man was walking now, and he had his thumb
out, trying to get a lift.

"Do we pick him up?" asked Estava.

"No, he'd recognize us," Jupe said.

Estava turned onto the highway and drove
south a block or two, then pulled into the
parking area next to a fish restaurant. The
boys watched through the back window.
They saw a van pull over and take Ramon
aboard.

"Dark Chevy van," said Jupe.

"Got it," said Estava.

They stayed two cars behind the van all
the way to Santa Monica. At Lincoln Boulevard the van shot up the exit ramp and

pulled over. Ramon got out and the van drove away.

Again Estava passed the dishwasher as if he didn't even see him. He zipped around a corner and stopped. The boys looked back.

Ramon was walking along with his head down and his shoulders hunched.

Estava turned back and followed, passing Ramon and parking to wait for him to go by, then following again. Ramon did not seem to have any suspicion that he was being trailed. He never looked at the gray car.

After a few blocks they came to a desolate area where the ground was scraped bare, as if someone had taken a giant razor to it.

"They've been tearing down old buildings along here," said Estava. "Probably it will be a business park. It's a cinch they won't build houses here. It's too close to the freeway. The noise is too much."

Ramon was just a shadow now, trudging across the barren ground toward some dark shapes beyond the cleared area. They were the shapes of houses—empty, ruined houses. Ramon disappeared between two of the deserted-looking places.

"We'd better get out and go after him on foot," said Jupe. He opened the car door.

Everyone jumped out. All four walked as

silently as possible toward the place where they had last seen the dishwasher.

"Where'd he get to?" Pete whispered as they stumbled into the blackness between the houses.

"Shh!" cautioned Jupe. "Look!"

There was a gleam of light ahead—a tiny line of brightness showing in one of the abandoned houses. The young detectives crept forward. One careful footstep after another, they crossed the ground until they were close enough to see that there was a window. Shutters had been closed over it, but light showed between several broken slats.

The freeway roared very close to the house, and a blast from the horn of a semi made them jump.

When the truck had thundered by, Jupe put his eye to one of the broken places in the shutter. He looked into a room where there was a bed and a lopsided bureau. A kerosene lamp burned on the bureau. Ramon was standing over the bed, looking down at the man who lay there. The man appeared to be unconscious. He lay partly on his side, his face turned toward the window, his mouth open a little and his eyes closed. Jupe saw a shackle on one bare ankle. A chain was attached to the shackle. The other end of the chain was fastened to a ring set in the concrete slab of the floor.

Jupe backed away from the window and motioned to his friends to move back with him.

"We've found Jeremy Pilcher," he whispered. "Now we've got to get him out of there!"

15

THE EARTH ROARS!

Ray Estava and the Three Investigators re-treated across the rough ground to another empty building. There they stopped to plan their next step.

"We could just bust in there and grab Pilcher," said Estava, "only that might not work if the guy who's holding him has a gun. If he *is* armed and he gets desperate enough, it could be the end of Pilcher."

"It could be the end of us, too," Pete pointed out. "Why don't we just find a phone and call the cops?"

"Okay," said Estava. "I'll go make the call. When the police get here and see the old man shackled to the bed and the other guy stand-ing over him, they'll know who the kidnap-per is, and I'll be off the hook.

"While I'm gone, you guys stay close to Pilcher, huh? I'd hate for anything to happen

155

to him now that we've found him."

Estava went off without waiting for the boys to agree or disagree.

"Maybe one of us should have gone with him," said Pete after the sound of his footsteps had died away.

"What for?" said Bob. "He knows how to call the cops."

"I hope he *does* call the cops," Pete said. "He has plenty of reasons to hate Mr. Pilcher. He could change his mind and leave us sitting here like stranded ducks."

"What would that accomplish?" said Jupe. "He knows we wouldn't sit here forever. He'll call the police. And he's right about keeping close to Pilcher. I don't like the way Ramon looks. He may be on the point of doing something desperate to Pilcher."

The boys stole back to the house where the lantern burned behind the shuttered window. Jupe looked through the gap in the shutter. Ramon was still beside the bed, still staring down at his prisoner. His cheeks were hollows in the faint light from the lantern. He looked as if he had been hungry too often in his life.

"Old man, you do not fool me," he told Pilcher. He shouted as if Pilcher might be deaf. There was no glass in the window, and the sound carried to the boys in spite of the noise of the freeway.

"You pretend!" Ramon bent and took hold of Pilcher's ankle. He shook the old collector. "You can hear me. I know it, so do not act the sick man with me!"

At the window, the Three Investigators were tense. Would Ramon hurt Pilcher? Would they have to break in before Estava could return with the police?

"I want the book!" Ramon leaned close to Pilcher's ear. "I earned that book. I paid for it with years of my life—years of disgrace, of prison. I would have shared with you, but you were so greedy, you wanted it all! It was you who told, wasn't it? You went to the police the moment you had the book in your hands. You said you knew who took it. They told me when they came for me that they had information. They arrested me. Me! Ramon Navarro! They put me in a cell like a common thief!

"You know what happened when they could not find the book in my room? They said I had sold it. They said it could only have been me, so I went to prison.

"I know where you went, Pilcher. To the place where you could fill your pockets and make yourself a rich man!"

Ramon turned from the bed. He twisted his hands together and paced the room.

Pete looked back in the direction where Estava had disappeared. Why didn't he come? What was taking him so long?

Inside the lighted room, Ramon stopped his pacing. He spoke again to the man on the bed. His voice was softer now, and the boys had to strain to hear. "Now you play for time," he said. "You think that girl of yours, she will be at the police until they find you. You think they will look and look until they come at last to this place, and there will be a rescue like in the cinema. No. I watch, and I see she does nothing. She calls the little boys to come so she will not be afraid in the dark. When she is still afraid she runs to her mother. The police do nothing. And you are still here.

"You know where you are, Pilcher, my old friend? You are in a place where no one comes and no one hears. I have much time. I can keep you until you tell me what I must know. Look!"

He strode to the shuttered window.

Pete gasped and flung himself sideways.

Bob scrambled off in the other direction.

Jupe pulled back. He tried to duck, but he was not quick enough. Ramon flung the shutter open. It swung out, almost hitting Jupe in the face.

For the tick of a watch Jupe and Ramon stared at each other. For a second Jupe could not move.

Then Pete grabbed Jupe and yanked him away from the window. The spell was broken. The boys ran, all three of them.

They heard Ramon shout. The shutter banged back against the side of the house. A door slammed.

Ramon was coming after them!

Jupe looked back. He saw the weapon in Ramon's hands. Not a gun. Ramon was brandishing a club of some sort. Jupe decided it was a baseball bat. He also decided that in Ramon's hands it was lethal. Ramon was not young, but he was nowhere near as old as Pilcher, and he was very husky.

Jupe ran still faster while Ramon shouted threats in Spanish and in English. The boys could not understand it all, but they knew that he called them sons of dogs. He told them that he would beat them into the ground when he caught them. Then he stopped yelling so he could run faster.

Pete let out a wordless whimper and ran to cover in the deeper darkness between two of the abandoned houses. Bob raced after him, and Jupe literally threw himself into the shadows.

Still Ramon came on. In a second he would have them; he would swing the bat.

But there were three of them. Surely the boys could wrestle the bat away from him and take him down.

Pete decided that it was too risky. Even if they won in the end, Ramon could brain one of them before they disarmed him.

Pete grabbed Bob's arm and tugged. He and Bob stumbled toward the back of the house. Jupe trotted behind them, looking back over his shoulder to see how close Ramon had gotten.

Too close, he thought.

Then Pete was beside him, pointing. A door! Pete had found an open door! They could get into an empty house and hide.

The three boys groped their way into the blackness inside the house. Jupe went with his arms out in front of him, for the darkness was so intense that it seemed his eyes must be shut.

Once they were inside, they turned to face the doorway, and Jupe saw the lighter darkness outside. He heard Ramon pause beside the house. His breathing was harsh. Jupe pictured him crouched near the doorway, listening, trying to catch some whisper of sound that would tell him where the boys were.

He moved at last. Jupe heard a single step, and then another. Jupe began to back off, to get away from the open doorway.

Step by slow step, he retreated until he felt a wall at his back. Then he moved to the side. Pete was next to him. Or was it Bob? It didn't matter, as long as they were all three together.

When he felt an emptiness behind him, Jupe knew he had come to another doorway. There was a second room behind the one that the boys had entered. Jupe stepped back through the doorway. His companions came after him. They were safe for the moment, but only for the moment. Ramon was at the outer door. He was listening, waiting for his quarry to move.

Jupe looked around, hoping for another door or a window, any way to get out of the house. He saw only blackness.

Estava! Where was Estava? Why didn't he come with the police?

Pete was right, Jupe thought bitterly. Estava had changed his mind. He had abandoned them. It was up to them now. They had to help themselves. They had to charge Ramon and get that bat away from him!

Suddenly the floor shook under Jupe's feet.

It was just a hint of movement, as if a truck had passed on the freeway.

Then the earth roared! The floor rose up. It settled, then rose again. The roar grew louder, louder. It filled the world so that there was nothing but the roar and the house tilting around Jupe. Lights flashed. The flashes were blinding, like lightning. The wires on the utility poles outside—they were shorting out!

Jupe fell, hearing the old house scream as timbers pulled away from timbers and nails were wrenched from wood.

Earthquake! It was an earthquake! Any second the old house would come down. The roof would pull away from the walls and fall in to crush them. They had to get out!

But Jupe could not get out. He could not even stand up. He lay on the heaving floor, his nails digging into the wood beneath him.

Any minute the house would collapse.

Jupe was trapped!

16
COMPLAINTS!

The shaking went on and on. Would it ever stop? Jupe clung to the floor, obsessed with the mad idea that he would fall off if he did not keep a firm grip on the boards beneath him.

He heard timbers groan and squeal around him. The roof was trying to pull away from the walls that held it up. There was a shattering, long drawn-out sound nearby and Jupe winced. Somewhere a wall was giving way. A house was coming down. Was it this house? Would Jupe and his friends be crushed—buried in debris?

The shaking stopped at last. Trembling, Jupe sat up. He saw a square of light in the blackness of the room, and he knew it was a window, and so he knew that the wall was still there. The house hadn't collapsed. Jupe was safe. So were Pete and Bob.

Pete spoke up in the darkness. "I hate it when that happens! I'll never get used to it—not ever!"

"Move to Illinois." Bob was trying to make a joke of it, but he sounded shaky.

Jupe staggered to his feet. When the shaking started, Ramon had been standing in the outer doorway with his bat in his hand. Now he was gone.

Jupe went to the door and looked out. He saw the air thick with dust, and he smelled the musty, dry-rot smell of old houses, but there was no sign of Ramon.

Car lights blazed on the freeway, but the noise was muted. The tireless, endless stream of traffic had halted. People shouted and horns blasted, but nothing moved.

With a shock, Jupe realized that he shouldn't have this unobstructed view of the freeway. Minutes ago there had been a house in the way. That house had changed its shape. It looked more like a lean-to shed. Three of the walls had collapsed, and the roof had come down. It leaned against the one remaining wall like a giant, tilted pot lid.

But that was the house where Navarro had imprisoned Pilcher!

"Oh, no!" Bob groaned. "He's buried—"

He was interrupted by a light. A car was

coming, bouncing across the cleared area near the wrecked house. Its headlights stabbed through the blackness and touched Ramon.

Ramon stood gazing helplessly at the remains of the old house. He looked around toward the approaching car. The headlights blinded him, and he did not see the second car behind the first one. The second car had red and blue lights flashing from the top. It was a police car.

Jupe grinned. The police had arrived.

Ramon turned to look back at the boys. He still had the baseball bat. The Three Investigators braced themselves. If he came at them, they would have to move fast.

But Ramon dropped the bat and started to run. In a flash he had disappeared beyond the fallen house.

The police car jolted to a halt. The doors flew open and two officers jumped out and raced after Ramon, shouting for him to stop.

The other car stopped and Ray Estava got out. He was moving almost as quickly as the policemen. "Mr. Pilcher!" he yelled, racing toward the wrecked house. "Mr. Pilcher! It's all right."

A voice came back—a high, cracked voice. "It is not all right! Don't be an idiot! A house just fell on me. Don't tell *me* it's all right!"

Incredibly, Jeremy Pilcher was still alive in that ruined place—alive and complaining!

The policemen reappeared. They had over-taken Ramon before he reached the freeway. He was handcuffed and he marched between the officers with his head down.

"That's the kidnapper!" Bob stepped to-ward the officers.

Ramon tried to yank free and kick, and Bob ducked away.

The officers put Ramon into the back of the squad car as Estava cried, "Don't worry, we'll get you out, Mr. Pilcher!"

"Don't be all night about it!" snapped the cranky collector.

At that point Estava remembered who he was and why he was there. He thought of his father, ruined by the old grouch in the wreck-age.

"Mr. Pilcher, drop dead!" he said. He stalked back to his car, got in, and did not do one more thing to help—not even when a third car came hurtling across the field with Marilyn Pilcher at the wheel.

"Estava must have phoned Marilyn," Pete guessed. "No wonder it took him half the night to get back."

Mrs. Pilcher was with Marilyn. She helped to restrain the girl when she tried to go in through the window in the one standing wall so that she could comfort her father.

"You leave it to us," said one of the two police officers. "We'll get him out."

"Get the lead out of your pants!" shouted Pilcher. "Don't stand there talking about it!"

The house creaked and groaned and threatened to come down completely.

The two policemen went in through the window, and the watchers outside held their breath. For the moment Pilcher was safe. The leaning roof and the one standing wall formed a sort of tent over the old collector. But there were often aftershocks following a quake. Even a mild one could bring the rest of the house on Pilcher and the rescuers.

There was no aftershock, but an officer soon came back out of the window. He scowled at the boys.

"The old man is chained to the floor," he said. "Nobody warned us." He went to his car and called in for help.

Firemen came after that. It took almost half an hour for them to arrive, but once they were on the scene, they went about the rescue of Jeremy Pilcher in an efficient way. Two of them climbed through the window and surveyed the situation. They called for a hacksaw. After they used the hacksaw, they needed a crowbar. The boys heard wrenching and heaving in the wreckage. Then a stretcher went in through the window. Shortly after, Jeremy Pilcher was lifted out.

By that time an ambulance was waiting. "Careful, you clumsy ox!" Pilcher cried as the attendants lifted him into the ambulance.

"Oh, Dad!" Marilyn got in to ride to the hospital with her father. "Dad, just this once take it easy, huh?" she said.

At that instant there was an aftershock. The earth rumbled briefly. The old house where Pilcher had spent his captivity collapsed completely into a pile of termite dust.

17
AN ANCIENT MYSTERY

The Three Investigators were ready and waiting when Dr. Gonzaga arrived at The Jones Salvage Yard a week later. As the professor from Ruxton drove them up the coast toward Malibu, the boys filled him in on their upcoming visit.

"You're going to like Mr. Sebastian," Pete promised. "He's a terrific guy. He used to be a private eye in New York. Now he writes mysteries out here. He's got this neat house that used to be a restaurant."

"And he's got a houseman from Vietnam," added Bob. "Hoang Van Don. You just call him Don. He's nice, but he's kind of weird about food. Some of the stuff he cooks is great, but some of it is—*bleaaah*!"

Following Jupe's directions, Dr. Gonzaga soon turned off the Coast Highway and drove slowly up a rutted canyon road to a big white-painted house.

"Hey, look!" Pete pointed. The house door was open and a very small girl stood on the porch. She wore a headband with a red feather stuck in it.

"Ah," said Dr. Gonzaga. "A little Indian girl. You didn't tell me about her."

"She's a new member of the cast," Jupe said, "and I don't think she's an Indian."

Dr. Gonzaga saw then that the child was Oriental. She smiled shyly and waved. Hoang Van Don came onto the porch and took her by the hand.

"Chumash princess!" he called. He pointed to the child. "Learning ways of early people in California."

As the visitors headed for the porch, other small children appeared from the house. All were Oriental and all wore Indian costumes.

"Small friends are project of East-West Fellowship," Don explained. "We find fun ways to teach American customs. When children go to school, they will be already Americans. Will find much acceptance from schoolmates."

"Kind of a Vietnamese Head Start project, huh?" said Bob.

"More fun than Head Start," Don told him. "Today we cook like Chumash Indians, make lunch with things we find on hillsides. Acorn cakes. Creamed dandelion. Also rosehip tea, good for digestion."

"Oh, no!" moaned Pete.

Don shooed the children into the house as Hector Sebastian appeared. Jupe introduced the professor. Mr. Sebastian hardly had time to shake Dr. Gonzaga's hand before Pete piped up.

"What about this creamed dandelion stuff?" said Pete.

The mystery writer chuckled. "Fear not, Pete. I've given strict orders. We are not Chumash children, and we aren't going to eat anything foraged from the hills! I went out this morning and bought some real food. We'll eat after you've told me about your case."

The boys looked relieved. They always survived Don's experimental meals, but they weren't anxious to munch on acorns or dandelions.

Mr. Sebastian led the way to a big room with a spectacular view of the ocean. This had been the main dining room when the house was a restaurant. Now it served as a combination living room, library, and office. When everyone was settled around the coffee table, Bob handed over his notes on the Pilcher case.

"Dr. Gonzaga has some details to add to these," he told the mystery writer.

Dr. Gonzaga nodded. "Read Bob's notes first. My part of the story concerns a really ancient mystery. It happened four hundred years ago, so there is no hurry about retelling the tale."

Mr. Sebastian began to read, tuning out the sound of children happily chattering in the kitchen. When he had finished Bob's account of the bizarre kidnapping of the collector, he looked up and laughed. "So Jeremy Pilcher was still griping when the firemen hauled him out after the earthquake!"

Jupe grinned. "The leopard can't change his spots! And Navarro is no angel, either."

"Navarro's wanted by the police in a couple of South American countries," said Bob. "He's a two-bit crook and he's spent lots of time in prison. Dr. Gonzaga has the scoop on the theft of the bishop's diary. That was the first time Navarro swiped something and got caught, but it wasn't the last time. And he's sure to go to jail again for abducting Pilcher."

Dr. Gonzaga opened his attache case and took out the leather-bound book that Jupe had found aboard the *Bonnie Betsy*. "It's

been confirmed," he said. "This is the missing diary of Bishop Enrique Jiminez, who
lived in Bogotá long, long ago. He was called
the bloodstained bishop because people
thought he was to blame for the mistreat-
ment of the Indians who worked the gold
mines and the emerald mines for the Spanish
conquerors. The clergy had so much to say
about the government of the Spanish colo-
nies that the bishop could hardly escape
blame.

"In his diary, however, the bishop wrote
that he was alarmed by the tales of brutality
at the mines. He wanted to investigate, so he
journeyed to one of them—an emerald mine.
It was a sort of strip mine—the Indians dug
on the surface, not down in a pit. They were
being treated horribly. The bishop hurried
back to Bogotá to pressure the Spanish governor into making changes to protect the
Indian workers. Before the governor could
act, there was a landslide in the mountains.
The mine that the bishop had seen was
buried."

Dr. Gonzaga began to read from the diary,
translating as he read. "Men have been digging for months. They try to clear away the
fallen earth, but it is very dangerous. There
are always more landslides. Now word has

come. There is a mutiny. The Indians refuse to dig more. Yesterday the governor gave the order; the mine will be abandoned. It is as well. The tears of the gods have caused too much weeping among men."

"Hmmm!" said Mr. Sebastian. "So the bishop wasn't a villain after all."

"He got a bum rap," said Pete.

"But what about the pages that are missing from the book?" Mr. Sebastian asked. "Do they have something to do with the mystery?"

"They have everything to do with it," said Dr. Gonzaga. "The exact location of the mine was lost after the landslide. However, from the position of these pages in the diary, we know they must have been an account of the bishop's journey from Bogotá to the mine. Any treasure hunter could retrace the bishop's route and go straight to Sogamoso. At the place where the Old Woman casts her shadow, he would find the mine. The Old Woman is a mountain in the Andes. The natives refer to the peak that way.

"The bishop's diary was in a private collection for many years. The owners couldn't have known what they had. Eventually a rare-book dealer bought the diary, suspecting that it might be a rich find. Before he could have the book examined by experts, it was stolen. The police were tipped off that the dealer's assistant had the book. They went to the man's room and found several rare documents that the fellow had taken from the shop, but no diary."

"Aha!" said Mr. Sebastian. "Was the assistant our friend Navarro?"

"Right," said Pete. "At first Navarro denied everything. Then he said an American had come into the shop and had walked off with the diary hidden under his jacket. The police didn't believe this, so Navarro went to prison."

"We have to guess what really happened," said Bob, raising his voice to be heard above a sudden gale of laughter from Don's kitchen. "Neither Navarro nor Pilcher is talking. We know from Marilyn that when her father was a sailor, traveling all over the world, he didn't just hang around ports when his ship docked. He traveled inland whenever he could. He was ambitious, always looking for an opportunity to get ahead. Somehow Pilcher met Navarro in Bogotá. Somehow Navarro had learned what the diary said—at least about the emerald mine at Sogamoso. Somehow the two schemed together to steal the book, and then it seems Pilcher double-

crossed Navarro. Navarro was arrested, and
Pilcher came back to the States with a whole
lot of money."

"Which means he found the emerald
mine," said Mr. Sebastian.

"It seems likely," said Jupe. "We think he
followed the route that the bishop described
in the diary. The diary isn't easy to read, but
Pilcher knew some Spanish and could have
puzzled out a few pages with the help of a
dictionary."

Dr. Gonzaga nodded. "You could have read
it yourself, Jupiter, with time and some reference books. Spanish hasn't changed that
much in four hundred years—any more than
English has. We can still read Shakespeare
with little trouble."

"And what was the diary doing on the
Bonnie Betsy?" Mr. Sebastian asked.

"We think Pilcher sailed down to Colombia
whenever he needed more emeralds," said
Bob. "The diary was his guide to the mine. At
some point he stopped making the trip;
maybe he got too old. He ripped out the
important pages and took them home to hide
them. I guess he left the diary on board
because he never liked to throw anything
away."

"So the man fueled his fortune with emeralds," said Mr. Sebastian, "and then his

former partner in crime showed up at his daughter's party. What a shock that must have been!"

"It brought on an angina attack," Jupe said. "Navarro recognized Pilcher in spite of the years that had passed, and Pilcher knew it."

Pete took up the story. "We figure Pilcher pretended to be resting while I was sitting with him, and all the time his mind was ticking away like mad. He knew Navarro would come after him, and he knew Navarro would want the diary. Pilcher wasn't about to give up his secret, so when he got his chance he locked me in the bathroom and burned the pages. Then he put that message into the computer for Marilyn. He wanted to tell her about the mine, but only if something happened to him."

"Stingy to the end," murmured Mr. Sebastian.

Pete went on. "Navarro came upstairs when no one was looking, and he snuck up on Pilcher just as the old man was going to let me out of the bathroom. Navarro put a pillow over Pilcher's face—maybe he just wanted to scare him. The first pillow split so he grabbed a second one. Pilcher passed out. We think Navarro got scared he'd killed the old man and decided to take Pilcher away with him and hope it would look as if Pilcher had disappeared on his own."

"How did he get Pilcher out of the house?" asked Mr. Sebastian.

"In the laundry cart," said Jupe, "under the dirty linens."

"Where else!" said Mr. Sebastian with a laugh.

Jupe continued, "After the party was over, Navarro had the job of taking the linens to the laundry. Before he got there he found that it wasn't just a body he was toting around. Pilcher was still alive."

"So it looked like this was Navarro's big chance to make his fortune," said Bob. "The vacant house near the freeway was a great place to keep a prisoner. No one could hear if he yelled. The police think Navarro must have camped out at that house a time or two before Burnside hired him. The guy who once lived there had some heavy machinery that had to be fastened down, and so there was that ring in the floor.

"Navarro didn't want Pilcher to die on him, so he saw that Pilcher always had food and water. Pilcher pretended to drift in and out of a coma so he wouldn't have to answer Navarro's questions. Navarro suspected he was faking, but he was afraid to put too much pressure on Pilcher. If Pilcher had a fatal heart attack, the mine would be lost forever."

"How is the old collector now?" Mr. Sebastian asked.

"He's recovering," Pete said. "It's a miracle, but he wasn't hurt when the roof came down."

"I can't believe that that house collapsed," said the mystery writer. "It couldn't have been such a severe earthquake. I was in New York last week. The papers hardly mentioned a quake out here."

"The epicenter was right off the coast, and we were in a really tumble-down old house," Bob told him. "It was severe enough, let me tell you!"

Pete wrinkled his nose. A strange smell was coming from the kitchen, and the voices of the Chumash "Indians" were subdued. Grateful that he didn't have to be an Indian, too, Pete continued tying up loose ends of the case.

"Pilcher was in the hospital for a few days," Pete said, "but he's a tough old bird and he's home now. Marilyn isn't going to marry that guy from Boston. But as soon as her dad's stronger, she's going to move back in with her mom full time. She figures he'll never change, and if she hangs around him too much she might turn out to be as mean as he is. She says things like, 'Money isn't everything.' That drives the old grouch nuts."

"And all that secret stuff about the emeralds was a waste of time." Bob's eyes were dancing. "It turns out that somebody else found the mine a few years ago. It's being worked today. It's about as secret as the Rocky Beach branch of the Bank of America."

Mr. Sebastian chuckled. "Serves those two crooks right!"

"Ray Estava got a new job at a downtown bank," said Bob, "and Ariago is lying low at the Becket store, maybe hoping Pilcher will forget about him. He was trying to date Mrs. Pilcher, and he didn't want Pilcher to know, so he hid when he saw Jupe arriving at Mrs. Pilcher's. Mrs. Pilcher was so embarrassed by the whole thing she didn't know what to do. She says she doesn't even like the guy, but she can't seem to discourage him."

"Some people won't take no for an answer," joked Mr. Sebastian. "Now, what about the ghost in Mr. Pilcher's attic? Have you any explanation for the footsteps you heard?"

"I don't," said Jupe, "but Mrs. McCarthy, the housekeeper, does. She says the ghost belongs to the little girl who used to live there with her rich aunt—the girl who was sent home in disgrace when a pin of the aunt's disappeared.

"The girl had a hard time after that because her family believed she might be a thief. Mrs. McCarthy went up to the attic after we left and did some searching on her own. She found this stuck in the folds of an old quilt in one of the trunks."

Jupe put a brooch on the coffee table—a gold brooch with red stones set in it. "Mrs. McCarthy thinks this is the pin the girl was accused of stealing. She thinks the aunt must have lost it while she was putting things away in the trunk. After she died, the trunk went to Mr. Pilcher along with most of the things in the house.

"We think the first intruder in the attic was Navarro. He was frustrated because Marilyn couldn't find the bishop's book, and he came looking—and wound up tackling me. But after that? Well, Mrs. McCarthy learned that the girl—woman now—died in an auto crash the day of Marilyn's engagement party. The housekeeper claims that the woman's spirit came back to find the brooch and show it so that people would know she didn't take it."

"Came back to clear her name," said Mr. Sebastian.

Jupe nodded. "But there must be another explanation. Nobody comes back. There are no ghosts."

"Of course not," said Mr. Sebastian.

Suddenly voices in the kitchen were raised in protest. A moment later Don appeared to announce that Mr. Sebastian's lunch was almost ready. The strange aroma that had seeped into the living room now assaulted everyone's nose. It reminded Pete of baked sawdust.

"Children do not eat acorn cakes," said Don sadly. "Do not want to be Chumash Indians."

"Oh?" said Mr. Sebastian.

"Not to worry." Don smiled. "I take children to Pizza Shack on highway. Pizza is great all-American food. Even better than acorns!"

Mr. Sebastian laughed. Between Don's cooking and the Investigators' cases, he never knew what to expect. What would they all come up with next?

THE THREE INVESTIGATORS
MYSTERY SERIES

NOVELS

The Secret of Terror Castle
The Mystery of the Stuttering Parrot
The Mystery of the Whispering Mummy
The Mystery of the Green Ghost
The Mystery of the Vanishing Treasure
The Secret of Skeleton Island
The Mystery of the Fiery Eye
The Mystery of the Silver Spider
The Mystery of the Screaming Clock
The Mystery of the Moaning Cave
The Mystery of the Talking Skull
The Mystery of the Laughing Shadow
The Secret of the Crooked Cat
The Mystery of the Coughing Dragon
The Mystery of the Flaming Footprints
The Mystery of the Nervous Lion
The Mystery of the Singing Serpent
The Mystery of the Shrinking House
The Secret of Phantom Lake
The Mystery of Monster Mountain
The Secret of the Haunted Mirror
The Mystery of the Dead Man's Riddle
The Mystery of the Invisible Dog
The Mystery of Death Trap Mine
The Mystery of the Dancing Devil
The Mystery of the Headless Horse
The Mystery of the Magic Circle
The Mystery of the Deadly Double
The Mystery of the Sinister Scarecrow
The Secret of Shark Reef

(*Continued on next page*)

CAR

Carey, M. V.

The Three
Investigators in
The mystery of the
cranky collector

CAR

Carey, M. V.

The Three
Investigators in
The mystery of the
cranky collector

$6.99

DATE	BORROWER'S NAME	
Johnson	Montel	
1-20	Jarrell	18
42152	M	

© THE BAKER & TAYLOR CO.